THREE AGAINST ONE

As the three warriors bore down on him, Nate King drew his tomahawk and knife. Two held lances and were not quite close enough to use them. But the third man had a bow and already had an arrow nocked. He let fly without taking aim.

The shaft whizzed past Nate's shoulder, convincing him it was certain death to meet their charge in the open. Spinning to his left, he sped toward the woods, and cover. The trio veered to intercept, them but Nate gained the undergrowth well ahead of them. An arrow thudded into a tree as he flew by, prompting him to tuck at the waist and dash into a cluster of saplings. On the other side was a small clearing, which he covered in long bounds.

Tall firs dappled Nate with shadows as he glanced over a shoulder. The warriors had just reached the clearing and were looking about in confusion. They had lost sight of him but not for long. The one in the middle pointed and all three leaped in pursuit like wolves after a fleeing elk. They didn't whoop or holler as warriors from most tribes were wont to do. Grimly earnest, they spread out, the archer in the center, an arrow notched and another in his mouth ready for swift use.

WILDERNESS

Trackdown

David Thompson

LEISURE BOOKS   NEW YORK CITY

Dedicated to Judy, Joshua and Shane.

A LEISURE BOOK®

August 2001   *gift 1-30-03 $3.99*

Published by

Dorchester Publishing Co., Inc.
276 Fifth Avenue
New York, NY 10001

ISBN 0-8439-4905-8

The name "Leisure Books" and the stylized "L" with design are trademarks of Dorchester Publishing Co., Inc.

Printed in the United States of America.

Visit us on the web at www.dorchesterpub.com.

Trackdown

Chapter One

In a cloudless sky hung the blazing sun at its zenith. Shimmering waves of heat rose from the parched land below, an arid plain that stretched for as far as the eye could see. Not so much as a whisper of wind stirred the dust.

In the distance a speck appeared. It slowly grew in size until it took on the proportions of a big man in buckskins. His broad shoulders stooped from fatigue, his movements wooden, he shuffled westward, ever westward, his gaze glued to the tracks he had been following for days now.

Crowning his mane of dark hair was a beaver hat. Hardly fitting headgear in that stifling heat, but it protected his head from the relentless sun. And it absorbed much of the sweat that would otherwise trickle into his green eyes.

In his right hand the man held a heavy Hawken rifle, custom-made for him by the famous Hawken brothers in their shop in St. Louis. Wedged under his wide brown leather belt were a pair of matching flintlock pistols. He also had an ammo pouch and a beaded possibles bag slanted across his wide chest. On his right hip hung a bowie; on his left, under his belt, was a tomahawk. Moccasins completed his attire.

Halting, the man licked his swollen lips, moistening them with what little saliva he could muster. Then he squinted against the harsh glare to scan the baked landscape ahead. He was so hot, he felt as if the blood in his veins were boiling. He wanted to lie down and rest, to curl into a ball and sleep for a week to catch up on all the rest he had missed. But the tracks drew him on, steadily on.

A tiny voice in the back of Nate King's mind chided him for being so foolish, for being on the go during the worst part of the day when it was wiser to move at night. But he had no choice. He couldn't follow the foot- and hoofprints in the dark. And the prints were the only hope he had of ever again setting eyes on his devoted wife and darling daughter.

Torment tore at Nate King's heartstrings as he thought of Winona and Evelyn in the clutches of their unknown captors. He tried not to think of what might have been done to them, of the horrors they might be enduring at that very moment. He tried to keep his emotions in check, but he had lived in the wilderness too long and witnessed too much cruelty and savagery to be optimistic about their prospects.

It didn't help that Nate partly blamed himself for their capture. He had left them alone when he went off with several Shoshones to explore a canyon. Enemies slew his friends, and he had been lucky to make it out alive. Lucky, except he found his loved ones and all the horses gone.

By the light of a torch Nate had studied the sign and learned that a band of ten warriors were responsible. They had snuck up on Winona and Evelyn while the pair were seated by the fire and jumped them. Winona had struggled fiercely but been overcome. Her footprints, left when they marched Evelyn and her westward, indicated that she had not been gravely hurt.

That had been five days ago. Five days of stifling heat, of burning sun, of restless, sleepless nights spent tossing and turning. Five days spent in utter dread that he would stumble on the grisly remains of two people who meant more to him than life itself.

Opening the possibles bag, Nate reassured himself that he still had three pieces of pemmican left. Three small pieces to tide him over for who knew how long. He took one out and bit off a morsel barely as large as an acorn. Sucking on it rather than chewing, he willed his tired legs to keep moving.

Nate supposed he should be thankful he was still alive. He had no water whatsoever, and he had survived the past five days only because those he pursued seemed to know every water hole in the region. Twice they had stopped at spots where no water had been apparent until Nate was right on top of it. The first time had been at a tiny spring in the middle of a rock field. The second time at a shallow tank concealed among gigantic boulders.

A man could get by without much food, but water was essential. No one could last long in such a hellish inferno without it. Regrettably, Nate didn't have a water skin. Fate forced him to rely on men he despised to keep him alive.

A water skin wasn't the only thing he lacked.

Glancing at his Hawken, Nate frowned. To save himself from those who slew his friends, he had used his powder horn to blow up a passage through a cliff. Now he was completely out of black powder. His rifle and both pistols were essentially useless. Several times he had considered discarding them, but guns didn't grow on trees.

David Thompson

Nate's gaze drifted to the tracks. For the umpteenth time he wondered who the warriors were. He was well west of his usual haunts, in territory never explored by white men, in an area no tribes were known to exist. Or so friendly Indians had told him. To the Shoshones, the Crows, and others, the region was bad medicine and they shunned it.

Nate didn't blame them. In addition to the scarcity of water, there was hardly any game. In five days all he had seen were a few birds, several lizards, and one snake. On spotting the latter, he had dashed toward it to dash out its brains, but the snake slithered under a boulder too immense for him to budge. Which was unfortunate. Snake meat was downright tasty.

So was horse meat, evidently, to the warriors he was after.

On the second morning out Nate had come across the butchered remains of one of the horses. The head and legs still had flesh on them, but the rest had been devoured down to the bone, including the internal organs. What made it especially strange was that Nate found no evidence of a fire. The warriors had eaten the poor animal *raw*.

Nate had never heard of a tribe doing such a thing. Not even the Apaches, who routinely ate horse flesh but invariably cooked it first.

The moccasin prints, too, were a puzzle. As every frontiersman worthy of the name was aware, no two tribes fashioned their moccasins exactly alike. The shape, the stitching, was always different. Nate was familiar with every style on the frontier, but he had never seen moccasins like these: slightly crescent shaped, with stitching so plain a five-year-old could have done it.

Squinting into the haze, Nate trudged on, pondering yet another mystery. The warriors had stolen seven mounts—but not once had they ridden them. The horses were being led in a string, which flew in the face of all logic. Why not use them to cover ground faster? Were the animals merely food?

Presently, huge boulders loomed before him. Some were monoliths dozens of feet high, thick slabs jutting skyward as if thrust into the earth by primordial giants. Nate drew closer, and stiffened at the sight of a score of large black birds circling above them. Buzzards! he realized, and broke into a lumbering run, his sore muscles protesting.

Welcome shade bathed Nate as he plunged in among the slabs. Weaving toward the vultures, he spied the reason they had congregated and felt a wave of relief wash over him. It was the carcass of another horse, not the body of Winona or Evelyn.

Nine winged scavengers were already gorging on the remains. One, perched on a pair of exposed ribs, craned its hideous head and hissed. Several immediately rose into the air with a ponderous flapping.

Nate intended to give them a wide berth. Then he noticed a sizable chunk of untouched meat attached to the sorrel's flank and his stomach erupted in a growl loud enough to be heard by the vultures. Two more vaulted into the air and struggled to gain altitude.

Shaking his head, Nate started to go around. He was hungry, yes, but not *that* hungry. He refused to countenance the idea. But he couldn't take his eyes off the chunk, couldn't stop thinking of how empty his stomach was, of how long it had been since he last ate a meal.

On an impulse, Nate turned toward the horse. Instantly, the rest of the buzzards vacated their prize, one passing so close to Nate's head, he could have reached out and swatted it.

His mouth watering, Nate squatted next to the body. The horse had been slain the night before, so the remains were relatively fresh. Only a few flies were buzzing about. He had to admit he had eaten meat in a lot worse shape.

11

David Thompson

Gingerly, reluctantly, Nate pried at the chunk with his fingers. When that failed to dislodge it, he resorted to his bowie. A single slash sufficed. Sniffing it, he winced as his belly lanced with sharp pangs.

As famished as he was, Nate still balked. He cast about for fuel for a fire but there was none. Closing his eyes, he took a tentative nibble. A shudder coursed through him. Not from revulsion, but from how delicious it was—soft, salty, delicious. Half afraid he would be unable to keep it down, Nate chewed a few times, then swallowed.

Nothing happened.

Rising, Nate continued on. Above him the buzzards pinwheeled, awaiting the chance to resume their feast. He sank his teeth in deeper, tearing off a mouthful, and it was all he could do not to wolf it. Taking his time, savoring the taste and texture, he chewed for minutes on end, until the flesh was gummy pulp that slid down his throat like silken candy.

It took Nate over an hour to finish. Smacking his lips in satisfaction, amazed at how invigorated he felt, he licked his fingers clean of traces of blood and gore. He was almost tempted to go back for more. Almost, but not quite. Every minute he dallied was a minute longer Winona and Evelyn spent captive.

The tracks angled to the northwest, toward bumps on the horizon that grew into a range of hills. Nate was elated to see patches of vegetation, for where there were trees and brush there had to be water. His pace quickened, and he prayed that at last the band was near its destination.

Nate covered another hundred yards and happened to look down. In midstride, he stopped dead. In his excitement, he hadn't noticed a new pair of tracks that came out of the north and paralleled the others. One man, alone. But what a man! Nate placed his right moccasin next to one of the footprints and was astonished.

The newcomer's foot dwarfed his by a good five inches in length and at least two inches in width.

Whoever made the new prints had to be a veritable giant.

Hunkering, Nate examined them more closely. The man had been barefoot, incredibly enough. Impressions along the ball of the foot hinted at large calluses, which in turn told Nate it was normal for the giant to go without footwear.

Shielding his eyes, Nate surveyed the low hills. From this far out they seemed as lifeless as the parched plain. The warriors were about ten hours ahead, he estimated, while the giant couldn't be more than eight.

Again Nate examined the large footprints. The toes were twice the size of his, the heel much wider and thicker than a human heel would be. The ground was too hard-packed to offer a clue to how much the giant weighed, but based on the size of the tracks, it had to be considerable.

What kind of man was it? Nate wondered, rising. He recalled his encounter with strange, hairy man-beasts years ago, and his more recent clash with a tribe of steely-thewed brutes in the lost canyon. The tracks he had just found bore no resemblance to either. He was dealing with something new, something few whites, if any, had ever run across.

Squaring his shoulders, Nate pressed on. Unbidden, the tales he had heard around campfires late at night filtered through his mind. Tall tales, the stock-in-trade of trappers and mountain men, who delighted in telling whoppers to outdo one another. Like the one Jim Bridger loved to relate about a forest of petrified trees filled with petrified birds that warbled petrified songs.

Some of the mountaineers insisted their stories were true. There was Old Abe Murdock, for instance, who claimed that back in 1820 or 1821 he had been out on the prairie hunting buffalo with some friendly Pawnees.

They came to a low rise and spotted a herd on the other side. Before they could get into position, however, enormous shadows flitted across them. Startled, Old Abe had glanced up and beheld a flock of what he described as the "god-awful giantest winged critters in all creation!" Hawklike monsters with twenty-five- to thirty-foot wingspans, gliding silently toward the herd.

As Old Abe gaped, the birds had wheeled above the unsuspecting buffalo. Then, voicing hideous shrieks, they had dived like osprey plummeting in among a school of fish. It was the young buffalo they were after. Abe swore that six of those birds lifted bawling calves up into the air and flew south with them, the beating of their wings almost loud enough to drown out the bleating of their terror-stricken prey.

Later, Old Abe learned that the Pawnees and other tribes knew all about the giant birds, and had given them names that generally meant the same thing. Birds of the storm, or Thunderbirds, as the Sioux called them, because they were usually seen in the spring and early summer when thunderstorms were most common.

Another mountain man, Ezra Templeton, liked to relate the time he ventured deep into the mountains of northern California. In a pristine lake high among the Cascades he had seen black salamanders more than five feet long sunning themselves on the shore.

Later that same day, Ezra had observed two deer, a buck and a doe, swimming across the lake. Without warning, the doe vanished, sinking straight down as if pulled from below. Not a minute later, the same thing happened to the buck, but it reappeared, struggling mightily. A couple of seconds passed, and a long black shape hove up out of the water, clamping its wide maw on the buck's throat. Both disappeared in a violent spray.

A true story, Ezra claimed.

Nate was convinced the wilderness hid many mysteries. The mountains and the plains were home to creatures that should have died out long ago, creatures of legend to the many tribes that now inhabited their haunts. Creatures most easterners would deny could ever exist.

Suddenly Nate stopped. The tracks of the giant veered off to the north. Any other time, his curiosity would compel him to learn their maker's identity. But Winona and Evelyn were his paramount concern.

Trudging toward the hills, Nate soon approached the foremost. Stunted trees and dry brush sprinkled the slope. The tracks led straight up, and from the top Nate enjoyed a panoramic vista of the surrounding countryside. Of particular interest were jagged peaks miles to the west, a row of mountains almost as high as the front range of the Rockies.

Nate scoured the intervening hills, his pulse jumping when he caught sight of stick figures midway to the peaks. A long row of men and horses, it had to be the warriors he was after! Encouraged, he jogged to the bottom and gave chase. But he soon tired and had to slow to a walk. The horse meat had not revitalized him as much as he would have liked. He was still weak from hunger and lack of water.

Water. At the thought, Nate realized how truly thirsty he was. His throat was as dry as a desert. It hurt when he swallowed. His lips were split, his mouth an oven. He would gladly give anything for a handful of cool, refreshing liquid.

The tracks wound past a second hill, and the one after that. Rounding the fourth, he blinked in bafflement, unsure if his mind was playing tricks on him.

A shallow gulch knifed across his path, dry except for a trickle of water down its center. It was hardly enough to drown an ant, yet at that moment, it was more inviting than all the gold ever mined.

Jumping into the gulch, Nate knelt and touched a finger to the water, fearing it would evaporate into thin air.

But no, his fingertip was moist! Facing upstream, he eagerly lowered his cheek into the rivulet and opened his mouth so the water flowed in. Greedily gulping, he swallowed again and again and again, drinking until he couldn't down another drop, until his belly felt bloated and he had a terrible ache in the pit of his gut.

Groaning, Nate rolled onto his back and smiled contentedly. He wanted to lie there until nightfall, drinking to his heart's content, but he was spurred by worry over Winona and Evelyn into sitting up and treating himself to a few more swallows, then heading out.

Nate consoled himself with the notion that there had to be a lot more water where the warriors were bound, enough for an entire tribe. He was pleased to note signs of wildlife: deer tracks, rabbit spoor, and farther on, antelope hoofprints. The worst of his ordeal, he flattered himself, was over. By midnight he would catch up to the warriors, free his wife and daughter, reclaim some of the horses, and light a shuck for home.

"Home!" Nate said the word aloud, letting it roll off his tongue, the mere sound comforting. He couldn't wait to set foot in his cabin again, to sleep in his own bed, to eat a leisurely meal at the table he had built with his own hands. Weeks had gone by since they left, weeks of enduring hardship after hardship. All because he had done a kindness for an old Shoshone.

The gravely ill warrior had sought him out and pleaded for him to grant a favor. A simple enough request, on the face of it: to escort the old man to a remote canyon where the love of the man's life had perished years ago so the oldster could be buried by her side. But unforeseen perils had arisen. Now the old warrior, his three sons, and a grandson were all dead, and Nate's loved ones were in dire trouble.

Nate's mother used to say that doing a good deed was its own reward, but bitter experience had taught

him that there were some good deeds better left un-
done.

The afternoon waned. On discovering a pile of horse
droppings, Nate pried at them with a stick, breaking
them open to gauge exactly how long they had been
lying there. He estimated six hours. So he was gaining.
But it would still be well past dark before he overtook
them.

His stomach began to growl nonstop. To ease the
pain, Nate ate a piece of pemmican. He was hiking
briskly along when he glanced at the tracks and noticed
something he had overlooked.

No wonder he was gaining. His wife's captors were
moving at a slower pace than before, as the lengths of
their strides clearly proved. They had often paused and
turned in one direction or another, as if scanning the
hilltops, as if they were wary of being discovered.

Nate thought of the footprints he had seen. Were the
warriors afraid of the creature that made them? Or was
there something else, something he was unaware of?
Perhaps another tribe. Speculation was useless. And it
didn't matter, anyway. *Nothing* would keep him from
rescuing his wife and daughter. Absolutely nothing.

The hills became higher, their slopes steeper, the vegetation thicker, as the sun dipped low enough to roost
on the stark mountains.

It wouldn't be long before nightfall, and Nate
couldn't wait. Darkness was his ally. It would hide him
when he reached their camp.

As the golden orb relinquished its rein on the heavens, the western sky was painted with striking hues of
scarlet, orange, and yellow, splendid splashes of color
more vivid than any painter's palette could ever repro-
duce. Gradually they faded and were replaced by gathering twilight, which in turn deepened by degrees as a
multitude of stars blossomed, twinkling and sparkling
like a swarm of ethereal fireflies.

Nate was more interested in a land-bound firefly at the base of the mountains. The warriors had made camp and had a campfire going.

That, in itself, was mystifying.

Since he'd started trailing them, not once had Nate come across charred embers or any other sign of a fire. Granted, the lack of wood on the baked plain had been a factor, but there had been withered grass and weeds, enough to roast the horse meat they ate. Yet they never bothered.

As peculiar as it sounded, Nate reached the conclusion that they preferred cold camps and cold meat, but here was proof to the contrary. Or was the fire yet another sign they were afraid of something? Had they kindled it to ward off whatever lurked in the surrounding wilds?

As if in answer, a strange cry brought Nate up short. It wafted eerily on a breeze that had sprung up, a keening, ululating wail that grew in volume and pitch until it was more akin to the piercing shriek of a panther. In all his born days he had never heard anything quite like it. But even more disconcerting was an answering cry from the northeast. There were two of them, whatever they were, and possibly more.

Nate hefted the Hawken, wishing he had black powder. The warriors who abducted his wife and daughter should have some; Winona and Evelyn both had powder horns.

Another half a mile brought Nate close enough to make out dancing flames and figures huddled around it. The fire was bigger than most Indians would kindle, bigger, even, than whites were wont to make. Yet another puzzle. In enemy country, war parties always lit small fires in sheltered nooks where they were less likely to be spotted.

Slowing, Nate slanted to the south to approach the camp from a direction they wouldn't expect. He strained for a glimpse of Winona and Evelyn but didn't spot them. He did see the five remaining horses tied in a string a stone's throw to the east of the warriors. Much too far away, in his estimation. Ordinarily, mounts were kept close to prevent them from being stolen.

The animals had been pushed to the point of starvation and exhaustion. Their heads hung low; their bodies were flesh and bone. Without plenty of grass and water, none would live another week.

An enormous pile of wood and brush had been gathered, five or six times as much as was needed to last the night. Crouching, Nate moved nearer and had his first good look at those he had been tracking.

They were short of stature and lean of build. The tallest was about six inches over five feet, the average a couple of inches less. Oval faces and high cheekbones were the rule. Their wiry frames were well-muscled, their skin bronzed from exposure to the sun. Except for one man who wore a headband decorated with blue beads, they had unadorned black hair that hung past their slim shoulders. Their clothing consisted of breechclouts and ankle-high moccasins rather crudely sewn from deer hide.

Every warrior was armed with a bone-handled knife in a plain sheath. In addition, some held slender lances, while others favored small bows. None had guns. Nor did he see any sign of the guns belonging to his wife and daughter—or their ammo pouches and powder horns.

As with their breechclouts and moccasins, their weapons weren't of very of high quality. By any standard, they were some of the most primitive Indians Nate had ever beheld. Oddly, except for two whose job it was to keep the fire going, the rest sat with their backs to the flames instead of facing the fire as was customary.

Each one of them had a weapon in his lap ready for prompt use.

Quite plainly, they anticipated an attack. Yet if that

were so, Nate asked himself, why had they built the fire up so high? And why had they left the horses so far away? No self-respecting Shoshone would ever make the mistakes they had.

Or were they mistakes? The firelight extended some fifty or sixty feet, making it virtually impossible for anyone or anything to get near them without being seen. And, too, the horses were placed in such a way as to invite being stolen. Maybe that was what the warriors wanted. Maybe they were hoping that whatever they were afraid of would take the horses and leave them be.

Nate eased onto his stomach. He was approximately a hundred feet out. Another ten yards and his breath caught in his throat, a rapturous tingle rippling down his spine. Behind the warrior with the headband lay two figures, on their side, partially covered by blankets. He couldn't see them clearly, but it had to be Winona and Evelyn.

Overjoyed, Nate started to circle to the west for a better view. He glimpsed raven tresses spilling from under the blanket, confirming it was indeed his wife, but her features were still hidden. He yearned to call out, to let them know he was there, and wisely suppressed the foolish urge.

One of the warriors feeding the fire took a limb and tossed it on. The flames leaped high, crackling noisily, and a spray of red sparks fluttered upward like newborn moths taking wing.

Off in the dark, something grunted.

Only Nate heard it. Swiveling his head, he discovered that someone else was spying on the camp. A vague two-legged shape had materialized out of thin air. Since all the warriors were accounted for, it couldn't be one of them.

Whatever it was, the thing grunted again, then advanced as silently as an Apache—right toward him.

Chapter Two

Nate King let go of his rifle, his right hand sliding to the tomahawk at his waist. He assumed the newcomer had spotted him, but the next moment the squat shape veered to the west, moving with a fluid ease belying its bulk.

In the gloom all Nate could tell was that the figure wasn't much taller than the warriors by the fire, but it was much broader across the shoulders and had an immense barrel chest and a wild mane of hair. He saw the figure stop and tilt back its head, then heard it sniff several times, as a bear or wolf might do.

The men ringing the fire were oblivious to its presence. Two of the horses, though, had straightened and were gazing into the darkness with their ears pricked. Amazingly, none of the warriors took heed.

The bulky figure squatted. It was holding something, a long club, Nate guessed, although he couldn't be sure. For the longest while it watched the Indians. Every now and then it sniffed again, as if it had caught a scent it was interested in.

Nate didn't budge, didn't scarcely breathe. He hoped the prowler would drift elsewhere so he could get on with rescuing his wife and daughter, but no such luck. The minutes dragged into half an hour. By then all the horses were peering toward it, yet still the warriors were blind to the danger.

No, not all the horses, Nate saw. Several were gazing to his right. Slowly turning his head so as not to draw attention to himself, he involuntarily tensed. Another bulky shape was twenty feet off, its attention likewise riveted on the warriors. So there were two, maybe more. But two *what*?

Nate's skin prickled. For all he knew, a bunch of them were about to attack the camp. Winona and Evelyn would be caught in the middle with no means of defending themselves. He debated trying to warn the warriors but decided they were apt to turn him into a pincushion with their arrows before he could make them understand.

Just then, to the northwest, another eerie scream rent the night. Instantly, the pair of bulky forms shot erect.

So did many of the warriors. Nervously fingering their bows and lances, they jabbered excitedly in an unknown tongue.

The figure on Nate's left departed as silently as it had appeared, circling around the fire and vanishing in the murk. A second later its barrel-chested companion sprinted off, skirting the firelight on the other side.

Nate grinned and rose onto his elbows. Now he could concentrate on the matter at hand—namely, how to spirit his loved ones to safety without either being harmed.

Ten against one were high odds. A diversion was called for, and Nate focused on the horses. They weren't hobbled—yet another blunder the warriors had made. A mistake he could capitalize on.

Staying well back from the rosy glow, Nate crawled to the right. One of the horses, a bay, looked right at him. He came to where the second bulky figure had been squatting and smelled an odor that reminded him of the awful reek of a grizzly den. His nose commenced to itch, and an urge to sneeze came over him. Quickly, he pinched his nose, but the urge grew and grew. Throwing his other arm across his face, he pressed against it to smother the sound that might give him away. But the urge faded, and he crawled on.

To the west another of those bestial cries echoed off the mountains and was mimicked to the north. Neither sounded close enough to have been either of the two creatures Nate had just seen.

The horses were growing increasingly restless. Some nickered and stomped, some moved back and forth as far as the rope allowed. It wouldn't take much to spook them, to scare them into breaking loose and stampeding right toward the war party.

All the warriors had stood. At last Nate saw Winona and Evelyn clearly. They had sat up, and the blanket was down around Winona's hips. She looked as if she had been through literal hell. Her raven hair was disheveled, her cheeks smeared with dust. Her dress was torn at the left shoulder and had another tear low down in the front. Yet despite her appearance, she held herself proudly, her chin jutting defiantly at her abductors.

It upset Nate profoundly to see her in such a state. But it upset him far worse to behold his darling daughter. Barely ten years old, Evelyn had the cutest of button noses and normally the sweetest of smiles. But at that moment she was clinging to her mother, her face and button nose streaked with grime, her smile gone, her lips trembling in fear.

An icy fury gripped Nate, a fury so overwhelming he

had to exercise every ounce of self-control he possessed to keep from charging in among the warriors like a Viking gone berserk.

Images flooded through him, memories of happy, tender moments with Evelyn; of holding her in his arms right after she was born; of her first halting steps; of her tiny hand in his when they went for walks down by the lake; of the countless nights he tucked her into bed and listened to her prayers. Nate was no different from any other parent. His children meant everything to him. His love for them was as boundless. He would sooner rip out an eye or tear off an arm than see one of them harmed.

To witness Evelyn's plight was almost more than Nate could bear.

The warriors had turned toward the towering mountains and continued to jabber. Their backs were to the string.

Rising into a crouch, Nate padded forward. Another twenty feet and he would raise a ruckus to send the horses into a panic, driving them toward the warriors. In the confusion he would whisk Winona and Evelyn out of there.

Some risk was entailed. They might be trampled. But they were so close to the fire, Nate deemed it unlikely. The horses were bound to avoid the flames and anyone near them.

About ready to make his move, Nate suddenly registered movement off to the right. He went prone as another brutish shape loped out of nowhere. It, too, stood staring at the camp.

The night was crawling with them.

Warriors added more fuel to the fire. The flames jumped higher and lit up the vicinity as bright as day.

The figure in the grass backed away, demonstrating there was a method to the warriors' blunders. Their large fire was intended to keep the creatures at bay, and it was working. But it made Nate's task all the harder.

A piercing cry from amid the peaks galvanized the darkling form into trotting in the wake of its fellows. As it turned, the firelight played faintly over its features. Grotesque features they were, savage in the extreme. In its knobby right hand was an exceptionally thick spear more crude than those of the warriors. Essentially, it was a five-foot length of sapling trimmed to a point at one end.

Nate was glad to see the thing leave, but his anxiety was rising. How long would the fire deter the creatures? How long before they gathered in sufficient force to make a concerted rush? He moved toward the horses, determined to see it through before there was another interruption.

Several more steps, and Nate began to uncoil. He cupped a hand to his mouth to shout. Simultaneously, to the rear, stealthy footsteps padded. He tried to whirl, but he had reacted too late. There was a swish, a jarring blow to the back of his head, and the world spun madly. His knees buckled of their own accord.

Nate lost his grip on the Hawken. Barely conscious, he felt iron fingers wrap around his left wrist, felt himself being dragged deeper into the darkness. He was a big man, well over six feet and in excess of two hundred pounds, but whatever had hold of him abruptly slipped rock-hard hands under both his arms and effortlessly slung him over a shoulder as if he were a sack of flour.

A rocking sensation ensued as Nate was toted off into the night. He attempted to straighten, to resist, but he couldn't muster the willpower. He heard a low groan and realized he was the one groaning, then he had the illusion of pitching into a bottomless well, a well so inky black no light penetrated.

He passed out.

How long Nate was unconscious he couldn't rightly say. The same rocking sensation revived him. His head throbbed horribly and his abdomen was in agony from being gouged by his captor's shoulder. Cracking his eyelids, he slowly turned his head to find out who had jumped him.

It was one of the barrel-chested brutes. They were in the mountains, climbing rapidly. Judging by the stars and constellations, they were traveling northwest. The man—if such it was—moved up the steep slope with remarkable ease and rapidity, considering how heavy Nate was.

Only its back was visible. Its body was massively built, a solid block of muscle from shoulders to hips. Powerful legs pumped like pistons, corded sinews bulging with every stride.

Nate's chin bumped against a rough hide the brute wore. A deer hide, he deduced, with a hole in the center for the head, reminiscent of the ponchos worn by Mexicans down in Santa Fe.

Turning his head the other way, Nate spied a glow to the southeast. It had to be the fire. By his best reckoning, it was over a mile distant. Anger spiked through him, resentment at the creature that held him. He had been on the verge of saving his wife and daughter and it had unwittingly thwarted him. Now the opportunity was gone.

Suddenly the heavyset figure halted. Nate thought maybe it knew he was awake, but it simply stood quietly for a minute or two. He nearly jumped when it threw back its head and gave voice to another of the keening, ululating cries he had heard so many times already. But up close the cry was vastly more unnerving.

The lungs that produced it couldn't be human. The throat that uttered it was capable of a range and pitch no man or woman could match. And the rumbling roar that punctuated it was akin to the roar of a grizzly, an earsplitting blast of thunderous magnitude.

To the southwest a different creature replied.

Grunting, the man-beast lumbered upward, breathing no more heavily than if he were toting a leaf.

Nate craned his neck for a glimpse of the thing's face, in vain. His hands were dangling down near its feet, which were huge and bare. He remembered the tracks he had seen and realized he had been wrong. A giant hadn't made them. It had been a creature exactly like this one. A hulking monstrosity sculpted of solid brawn.

Where did it come from? What did it aim to do with him? Something told Nate that trying to talk to it would be futile.

The thing reached a wide grassy shelf, walked a few yards, and roughly tossed Nate to the ground. Rolling onto his back as he landed, Nate peeked at the creature. It was gazing to the southwest, and it was easy to guess why: It was waiting for the one that had answered its cry. Others might converge too.

Nate had to escape before they showed up. Cautiously, he roved his right hand along his belt. One of his pistols was missing, but he still had his bowie and the tomahawk. Sliding the latter from under his belt, he glanced toward the edge of the shelf, then at the man-brute's broad back.

Making no noise whatsoever, Nate slowly rose. He elevated the tomahawk and went to take a step.

Snarling viciously, the creature spun. Bathed in the pale starlight was a hideous countenance. Beady, dark eyes flashed with primal spite above extraordinarily wide, flared nostrils. Thick lips were pulled back from long, tapered, teeth more fitting for a wolverine. It had no forehead to speak of, its beetling eyebrows a hairline below a tangle of curly, reddish hair. Fast as thought, it raised a thick spear and lunged, driving the point directly at Nate's heart.

Nate threw himself to the right. The thrust missed, but the creature pivoted and pounced, arcing the spear in an overhand blow to transfix him from sternum to spine. Sidestepping, Nate saved himself, then buried the tomahawk in the man-brute's thigh.

A sinuous tongue flicked from the man-thing's wide maw as it uttered an enraged hiss. But the wound didn't faze it. Changing tactics, it swung the spear like a club, seeking to batter Nate into submission.

Ducking, weaving, dodging, Nate avoided the flurry. When an opening presented itself, he sliced his tomahawk into the creature's upper arm. But again it had no effect, other than to cause the abomination to rush him with renewed vigor.

In the swirl of conflict, Nate lost track of where he was in relation to the edge of the shelf. So he was all the more startled when he darted to the right to keep from having his skull split and his foot slipped on the steep slope. Momentum and gravity conspired to pitch him over the rim. He tried to stay upright, to keep his balance, but his right leg swept out from under him and he was sent tumbling toward the bottom.

Nate bounced and rolled, out of control and gaining speed. A ponderous tread warned him the creature was after him, that when he stopped rolling it would be on top of him before he could stand.

Brush crackled as Nate plowed into a thicket. It slowed him but didn't stop him, and he hurtled out the other side with the creature still in pursuit. Desperate to stop, to regain his feet, Nate dug his elbows and heels into the earth in a bid to end his mad descent. Without warning the ground gave way beneath him, and he dropped like a rock through thin air. A bone-jolting impact knocked the breath from his lungs and he lay on his side, too dazed to move. Dimly, he heard a squawk of surprise, heard the rush of a body, and then, from below, a distinct thud and the crunch of bone.

Rallying his strength, Nate rolled over—and wished he hadn't. His right hand and right leg flailed at empty space. He was teetering on the brink of a ledge, and had it not been for a spur of rock he grasped, he would have shared the man-brute's fate.

In a twinkling Nate's head cleared and he took stock. He had dropped over a cliff and was suspended ten feet below the crest. His pursuer had fared far worse. Seventy feet below, its bulky form was sprawled amid jagged boulders, dashed to ruin.

There, but for the grace of the Almighty, would be Nate. Swallowing hard, he carefully shifted so he could sit up, his back to the cliff. He groped the wall, seeking purchase but finding none.

Nate dared not attempt to stand. As narrow as the ledge was, the slightest misstep would reap fatal consequences. His best bet was to sit there until dawn, until he could better assess the situation. But that entailed spending the rest of the night clinging to his precarious perch. As tired as he was, staying awake posed a challenge.

To the southeast the campfire glowed, a bit nearer now, but it might as well be on another planet for all the good it did him. Tears of frustration welled up in Nate's eyes as he thought of how close he had been to Winona and Evelyn.

A check verified that the bowie hadn't slipped from its sheath but that the other flintlock was gone. Now Nate had no guns at all. He had managed to hold on to the tomahawk, and he slipped it under his belt to free his other hand. Propping both palms against the ledge, he slumped in despair.

Life could be so cruel. A man never knew from one day to the other what the next would bring: happiness or hardship, peace of mind or scrapes with death. He had been enjoying a quiet, peaceful existence with his family until the old warrior showed up and catapulted him into the depths of a living nightmare. What had he done to deserve this? What had his wife done? Or Evelyn? Nothing whatsoever.

Calamity was no respecter of persons. It beset the rich and the poor, the powerful and the powerless, without regard to one's wishes. No one in their right mind *wanted* tragedy to befall them. It just did. Certainly, some people brought it on themselves, but more often than not, hapless innocents were caught up in events they couldn't resist. Witness his family.

As with calamity, so with death. Graveyards were testimonials to the fact that the Reaper did not play favorites. Death came to everyone in its time. All a person could hope to do was stave it off as long as possible.

Nate had staved it off more times than most. He had wrested his homestead from the wilderness, defying the elements and hostiles, pitting his wits and his thews against adversaries of every stripe, and he had always come out on top. In recent years he had been relishing the fruits of his labors, and had grown complacent and soft. He had forgotten the great law of survival. He had forgotten that the Reaper forever lurked in the background, waiting, always waiting. He had forgotten that a man could never, ever let down his guard or those he cared for most would suffer for his carelessness.

Glumly, Nate stared at the distant fire, wondering what his wife was thinking, what she was feeling. Did she imagine he had forsaken her? Abandoned her? Did she believe he was dead? His despair worsened, and a tear trickled down his cheek.

Wiping a sleeve across his face, Nate chided himself for being weak. What was it he had repeatedly told his children when they were small? Where there was a will, there was a way. So long as the spark of life animated him, he mustn't give up, he mustn't give in to helplessness and self-pity.

Closing his eyes, Nate rested his head against the cliff. Weariness gnawed at him, at every fiber of his being, compounding his sorrow. He thought of his son, Zach, and Zach's wife, Louisa, and was glad they had not been at their cabin when he stopped en route to the canyon to ask if they wanted to go along. If they had, both might be dead, or Louisa might be held captive along with the others.

Nate could never quite get used to having a son who was married. Within a year or so Zach and Lou planned to give him a grandson. He was barely forty, and he'd be a grandfather! It would be nice, though, to cuddle the child while rocking it to sleep in front of the fireplace. Children were one of life's main delights, their gaiety and—

Abruptly aware that his body was sliding over the edge, Nate jerked back. His eyes snapped open, his heart pounding like a blacksmith's hammer on an anvil. He had almost dozed off! Another few seconds and it would have been all over.

Shaking his head to clear it, Nate winced at the discomfort it provoked. Reaching up, he was surprised to find that he still had his beaver hat. Underneath was a nasty bump where the heavy spear had struck. The hat had cushioned the blow, and might be the only reason his head had not caved in like an overripe melon.

Staring at the fire, Nate whispered to himself, "I'm sorry, Winona. I'm truly sorry." He couldn't help feeling that he had let her down, even though he couldn't be blamed for what had happened.

Nate broke out in goose bumps as a strong gust of chill wind buffeted him. It promised to become a lot colder before dawn. He considered stretching out flat on the ledge to be less exposed to the wind, but he discarded the idea. If he was too comfortable, he might doze off again.

To occupy himself, Nate reflected on his life. On his trek west from New York City when he was eighteen at the urging of an uncle later slain by Utes. On the first time he set eyes on Winona and been mesmerized by her beauty and charm. On the journey they made to the Pacific Ocean, walking hand-in-hand on a pristine beach while watching the surf roll in.

Such tender, romantic moments were doubly precious because of the many times they had been separated. Especially during the years he had spent as a free trapper, when he was gone for months on end.

There were men who liked to joke that women were a mistake on God's part, that they were peculiar and contrary and good for only one thing. Nate didn't agree. Winona had proven herself his equal in every respect that mattered. Granted, she wasn't as strong physically, but she possessed an inner strength that rivaled or surpassed his own. As for her intelligence, she was smarter by half. At one time it would have embarrassed him terribly to admit it. Not now. He was proud of her savvy, just as he was proud of her deep inner beauty and sterling character.

If Nate had learned anything from two decades of having a wife, it was that women deserved to be treated with high regard, not as simpletons or tarts.

Nate grinned, recalling the last intimate interlude they shared shortly before they left. His eyes closed and he mentally relived every moment. How he would love to be back in their bed, her arms wrapped tight around his neck!

With a start, Nate straightened and gripped the edge. He had done it again! He had nearly fallen asleep. Annoyed at his lapse, he slapped his cheek several times to ward off lingering drowsiness. About to smack himself a final time, he froze when a grunt sounded from somewhere above.

Nate looked up. One of the creatures was up there, probably the same one that had answered the dead man-brute's cry. It gave voice to a series of guttural sounds and was answered by another.

There were two, then, and they were hunting for the dead one. Bracing for the worst, Nate put a hand on the Bowie and the tomahawk. But what use would his weapons be? Once the pair spotted him, all they had to do was drop a boulder or log over the side and he was a goner.

Their voices drew closer and closer, and just when Nate was convinced they were right on top of him, another wailing shriek arose from higher up the mountain.

The voices faded. The creatures had gone, but odds were they would be back.

Staying there until daylight was no longer an option. Nate twisted so he could hike his right knee up onto the ledge. Exercising as much care as was humanly possible, he brought his other knee up, then pressed against the cliff and slowly stood.

Another strong gust buffeted him, and for a fleeting instant Nate thought it would push him off. Spreading his arms wide, he ran his hands over the rough surface but once again couldn't find any handholds.

Raising his arms overhead, Nate saw that the rim was only a couple of feet beyond his fingertips. He might be able to jump and grab hold, but if he couldn't quite reach it, if he slipped, his doom was sealed.

Nate scanned the ledge. To his left it ended at a sheer drop-off twelve feet away. To his right it seemed to go clear across the cliff. Maybe, just maybe, it was closer to the rim farther on.

Taking a deep breath, Nate sidled northward. He hugged the rock face, moving one foot at a time, a few inches at a time. A turtle could have gone faster, but a turtle didn't have to worry about loose stones or shifting its weight at the wrong moment. Or the wind, which gusted with increasing force.

The cliff, Nate learned, curved somewhat, the ledge narrowing at the point where a vertical rock ridge or fold protruded just enough to bar his way unless he was willing to loop an arm around it and pull himself past.

Nate hesitated. Dirt had been raining from under the ledge, suggesting it wasn't as solid as it appeared. And the farther he went, the more dirt fell. It could well be that on the other side of the fold the ledge was too weak to support him.

His mouth had gone dry, his palms were sweating. Wiping first one hand and then the other on his buckskin shirt, Nate inched forward and slid his forearm along the wall, over the protuberance. Every nerve jangling, he did the same with his right leg. He couldn't see his right foot, but he felt the ledge under his moccasin and tested whether it would hold him by stamping on it as hard as he could. It held firm.

Now came the moment of truth. Nate placed most of his weight on his right foot and eased past the fold, his left foot sliding along behind him. He smiled, for it had gone well, but his jubilance was short-lived.

At the exact moment that Nate was poised precariously over the void, at the selfsame second he was most off balance, the ledge under his right foot began to crumble from under him.

Chapter Three

"I'm scared, Ma," Evelyn King said, clinging to her mother.

So am I, Winona King thought, but she did not say so aloud. She had to be strong for her daughter's sake. She must not give voice to the true depths of her anxiety and misery. She must not let on that she was terrified of what the future held in store. "Be brave, little one," she counseled, stroking her child's hair.

"I'm trying. I really am." Evelyn's wide eyes were on the ten men on the other side of the fire. "What's out there, do you reckon? What has these warriors so spooked?"

"I do not know," Winona confessed. The unearthly shrieks were like none she had ever heard. They were as much a mystery as their captors.

"Whatever it is, at least it's far off."

Winona was not so sure there was only one. And some of them might be a lot closer than anyone else suspected. She had noticed the horses staring fixedly into the darkness with their ears pricked. Something was close by. Something that unnerved them, that caused them to whinny and stomp. "We should try to get some sleep," she said.

"Are you kidding? I can't sleep with all that's going on."

Neither could Winona, but they had to try. They both were bone weary and starving. They had been walking for days, on the go from dawn until dusk, and the only food they had been given were strips of raw horse flesh. The first time, she had nibbled at it but felt too queasy to eat. The second time, she fared better and downed the entire strip. So did Evelyn. But that had been two days ago, and they had not eaten anything since.

Evelyn looked up at her. "Do you still think Pa will come? Do you still think he will find us?"

"Yes," Winona declared, although in her heart of hearts grave doubts afflicted her. Nate's love, his devotion, were as profound as her own. Were he alive, he would let nothing stand in the way of reuniting them. *But is he alive?* was the question uppermost on Winona's mind. Nate was an outstanding tracker. It shouldn't be taking him so long to catch up. Initially, she had thought he would show after a day or two, and when he didn't, she began to worry that he had not made it out of Bear Canyon.

The horses, Winona observed, were staring to the east now. She peered into the darkness and had a fleeting impression of motion, of a commotion of some sort. But she could just as well have imagined it. In a short while the horses lost interest and hung their heads in abject exhaustion.

Evelyn had closed her eyes, a cheek on Winona's chest. Cradling her, Winona rocked back and forth as she had so often done when her daughter was younger. "My sweet little darling," she forlornly whispered, choking back tears. *Strong!* she scolded herself. She must be strong!

The warriors were filing back around the fire. Their leader, the man with a beaded headband, sat down next to her, as he always did. He said something to her in his tribe's tongue and pointed at the mountains, apparently explaining about the shrieks, but none of the words were familiar, so all she could do was shake her head to show she didn't understand.

Gesturing at her, the warrior with the headband patted a bare spot on the ground. He drew a figure with his finger, a broomstick with a circle on top, then tapped his chest and indicated each of his companions.

"It stands for your war party," Winona said, nodding. "Go on." Even though the man would not understand her words, he was intelligent enough to get the gist of what she was saying.

The warrior drew a second figure. He took his time, adding much more detail, and smiled when he was done. It had a wide body, big feet, and an oversized head with exaggerated fangs. And it was holding a club or spear. Touching it, he shifted and pointed toward the mountains.

"That is what has been making those terrible cries?" Winona said. It explained why the warriors had made the fire so big, and why they jumped whenever another screech pierced the night. Placing her thumb on the figure, she asked, "What? What?" in their tongue.

Winona had been striving her utmost to communicate. Initially, she had tried her own language, Shoshone, as well as sign language, English, the Flathead tongue, a smattering of Nez Percé and Crow tongues, even some Sioux and Pawnee she had picked up here and there. All it earned were blank stares.

The warriors reminded Winona of tribes she had run into on the Pacific coast. Tribes who were ignorant of sign, the well-nigh universal language of the prairie and

37

Rocky Mountain tribes, and who had so few dealings with other tribes, they spoke no tongue but their own.

Once that failed, Winona tried a new approach. Whenever the opportunity had presented itself, she pointed at things and the leader told her what they were in his language. She couldn't string whole sentences together yet, but she would be able to before too long.

The man with the headband was named Ish-kay, which meant Hawk, as he had demonstrated by pointing at a red hawk soaring high in the sky and smacking his chest while repeating the name over and over. In his thirties, he had a friendly manner, but not so friendly he would let her go.

Each morning Winona pointed eastward and expressed her wish to leave, and each morning Hawk made a stern gesture of disapproval. Twice, early on, she had tried to escape, and they had caught her and dragged her back. Except for those occasions, they always treated Evelyn and her kindly. They had not abused her, had never hit her.

Another warrior was named Stone. He was Hawk's close friend and watched over them when Hawk was busy with others.

A third man, Broken Stick, Winona disliked intensely. He always leered at her with a hungry look in his eyes that had nothing to do with food. To the other men he was arrogant, even bullying, and the only one who seemed able to keep him in line was Hawk.

An older warrior, Winona had gleaned, was called Antelope. Or had a name that had something to do with antelope, since Hawk had pointed at antelope tracks, then at the man, over and over.

A fifth warrior was His-tas-ta, which, as near as Winona could tell, meant Growing Grass.

The others had names more difficult for Hawk to explain, although he had tried. One was possibly Stars at Night. Another was Runs Slow, or maybe Moves Slow.

Winona had also learned their words for horse, fire, sky sun, deer, rabbit, knife, bow, and scores of others. She knew the word for food and water, for hungry and thirsty. Now she touched the figure Hawk had sketched of the thing with the fangs and repeated in their tongue, "What?"

Hawk leaned toward her and whispered, "Dabi-muzza."

It was hard to say which shocked Winona more, the outright terror in his tone or the fact that the words were somehow familiar. She was positive she had heard them before, but where? Before she could give it much thought, Broken Stick hunkered in front of Hawk. They conversed awhile, Broken Stick becoming agitated enough to jab a finger at Hawk and raise his voice in anger. Three times Broken Stick pointed at her. Try as she might, she couldn't make sense of the dispute because they were talking too fast.

Finally Hawk grew harsh with the bully, and Broken Stick rose and moved away, pouting like a five-year-old. The gaze he threw at Winona simmered with spite. She had no doubt that if he were the leader, she would not be treated kindly at all.

Hawk touched her shoulder. He pointed at Broken Stick, tapped the figure of the fanged ogre, then pointed toward the mountains and said a sentence slowly for her benefit.

The only words Winona understood were "hungry" and "Sa-gah-lee," which, as she understood it, was the name of their people. Roughly translated, it was "Great Ones" or "Mighty Warriors."

It made no sense. Was Hawk saying they had argued over eating a meal? What did that have to do with her?

"I don't like that man, Ma."

Winona looked down. Evelyn was glaring at Broken Stick, who returned the favor. "I thought you were asleep."

"With all this ruckus? No, I was thinking about Pa, hoping he'll come soon. I'm so hungry, so tired. And I'm afraid something terrible will happen."

"I will not let anyone or anything hurt you," Winona vowed. Even if she had to give her own life to keep her promise. "You will be fine."

Evelyn sat up. "I'm a big girl now, Ma. You don't need to spare my feelings. I know we're in bad trouble. I know we might wind up dead."

"Big girls never give up hope, Blue Flower," Winona said in Shoshone, using her daughter's Shoshone name. In English she added, "And neither do Kings. We must stay alert and be ready to escape when we have the chance. Eventually they will let down their guard."

"You've been saying that for days now," Evelyn said, idly fiddling with one of the red beads on her buckskin dress. Usually she preferred to wear dresses typical of white girls, garments the family bought or traded for at Bent's Fort and elsewhere. But whenever they went off into the wilderness, Winona insisted she wear something more fitting, more durable.

Winona never let on, but it bothered her, a lot, that her own flesh and blood, her only daughter, had little interest in Shoshone ways, in Shoshone customs. Her son Zach, on the other hand, always dressed as a Shoshone, and for years his ambition had been to be a prominent Shoshone warrior.

Evelyn didn't seem to dislike the Shoshones; she delighted in visiting them as much as the rest of the family. But her ambition was to one day go to Kansas City or St. Louis to live. "Or maybe even New York," Evelyn once mentioned. "Pa's from there, and I've always hankered to see where he grew up."

If that day ever came, it would be the saddest of Winona's whole life.

Runs Slow and Stars at Night were adding firewood

and dry brush to the fire. Evidently they intended to keep the flames roaring all night.

Winona's stomach grumbled, and she hungrily studied the horses. She never thought she would see the day where she'd seriously consider eating horse meat, but starvation had a way of altering a person's outlook.

"Ma, what if we never do get away?" Evelyn asked.

"You must have hope, remember?"

"I know. I know. But what if we don't?" Evelyn persisted. "What will they do with us? Kill us?"

"If that was all they had in mind, they would have done it long ago," Winona said. "No, I think one of the warriors will take us into his lodge, take us for his own."

"Take you for his wife, you mean?" Evelyn said, appalled. "But he can't! You have Pa! It wouldn't be right."

"No, it would not, and I will deal with it when the time comes." Winona refrained from mentioning the other possibilities. Some tribes made slaves of their captives and worked them to death under grueling conditions. Some sold or traded captives to neighboring tribes for horses and guns and whatnot. Which was a lot better than what the Apaches and a few others did; they were notorious for torturing those they caught.

Evelyn was indignant. "I'd like to see them try, Ma! I'll raise a fuss if they make us live with some warrior. Honest to God, I will! I'll make him so miserable, he'll throw us out of his lodge and want nothing to do with us."

"Such a temper," Winona said, smiling. Exactly like her father. In so many respects, Evelyn was much more like Nate. "But we must keep our wits about us. We must not provoke them if we can help it."

"I don't care how riled they get. They had no right snatching us, Ma. If Touch the Clouds knew, I bet he'd lead a hundred warriors here to wipe them out."

Touch the Clouds was Winona's kin and war chief of the Wind River Shoshones. A giant of a warrior who had counted more coup than any living Shoshone, he was particularly fond of Blue Flower. "I bet he would, too," Winona agreed.

Down from the mountains wafted another inhuman cry. The warriors stopped whatever they were doing to listen.

Hawk appeared worried. Taking Stone and Antelope, he went to the horses and cut the rope. Then they did a strange thing. Each man led a horse to a different spot along the perimeter of firelight and tethered it. When they were done, there was a horse to the north, south, and east, and two to the west.

"Why did they do that, Ma?" Evelyn wanted to know.

"I have no idea," Winona admitted.

"Wouldn't it be smarter for them to bring the horses in close so nothing happens to them?"

That it would, Winona mused. It was almost as if they had staked the horses out as bait. Or, given how scared they were, as an offering to whatever it was they were so afraid of.

The notion wasn't as preposterous as it sounded. Her own people indulged in the practice at a lake high in the Rockies. It was reputed to be the home of a ferocious aquatic beast that in winters past overturned canoes and devoured those who fell in the water. One day long ago an enterprising warrior hit on the idea of appeasing the beast by offering it a dead deer. So now, whenever anyone needed to cross the lake, a doe or buck was thrown in before they started across.

Hawk returned and squatted. Unslinging his ash bow, he took an arrow from the quiver on his back and nocked it to the sinew string.

Winona tapped his elbow, and when he turned, she placed a finger on the sketch of the ogre, then pointed at the horses and said the word for "eat."

42

"Yes," Hawk said, and added considerable detail, little of which Winona could comprehend. He ended by encompassing the entire war party with a sweep of his arm, then tapping the ogre while chomping and grinding his teeth.

"What's he going on about?" Evelyn asked.

A chill crept over Winona as a horrific insight dawned. "He can't be saying what I think he's saying," she said softly, more to herself than her daughter. To confirm it, she pointed at each of the warriors in turn, then at the sketch, then imitated eating, as he had done.

To her consternation, Hawk replied, "Yes."

Winona surveyed the encircling darkness in budding dread. The ogres *ate* humans. Yet based on the admittedly rough sketch, they were human themselves, or human-*like*. And if that were true, they were cannibals.

When Winona was a small girl, she had delighted in staying up late to listen to the stories her elders told. One, especially, she never forgot. It had terrified her like no other, giving her many a sleepless night. It was a legend as old as the Shoshones themselves, a legend passed down from generation to generation and supposedly based on true events.

The legend of the red-haired cannibals.

As the tale went, the cannibals were the scourge of the mountains. For hundreds of winters they preyed on the Shoshones and other tribes, stealing women and children in the dead of night and waylaying lone warriors in the woods. When search parties were sent out, all they ever found were gnawed bones.

One day a chief called White Feather decided enough was enough. He gathered warriors from every Shoshone village and set out to exterminate the cannibals. White Feather tracked them to caves in a remote valley, where a tremendous battle was fought. Many Shoshones were slain, but they succeeded in driving the red-haired cannibals off. It was said the cannibals drifted into Paiute country and for many winters preyed on them as they had on the Shoshones.

The Paiutes claimed to have destroyed them. But from time to time new reports surfaced, accounts from the Crows, from the Nez Percé, the Flatheads. Reports hinting that the cannibals had survived, but in greatly reduced numbers.

Winona looked at Evelyn, at a cluster of red beads on her dress. Getting Hawk's attention, she placed her finger on one of them, then touched her hair, and finally touched the sketch.

"Yes."

The legend *was* true, then. Winona's childhood fears were reborn in a rush of blind terror, which she overcame by sheer force of will.

"What is it, Ma? Tell me."

Composing herself, grinning to reassure Evelyn all was well, Winona draped an arm around her shoulders and pulled her close. "It's nothing for you to fret about," she fibbed. She couldn't bring herself to reveal the truth.

"What's doing all the screaming? Did he say?"

"No. Wolves, I suppose." One fib was leading to another.

"They don't sound like any wolves I've ever heard," Evelyn said. "Or any painters, either."

"Whatever they are, the fire will keep them at bay," Winona remarked. "So I suggest you lie back down and try to sleep."

"Ahhh, do I have to? I told you I'm not sleepy."

"Yes, you have to." Winona held the blanket so Evelyn could crawl underneath and tucked it around her chin. "There."

"I don't need a cover. It's hot enough as it is being so close to the fire. What about you? Aren't you turning in?"

"I'll lie down in a bit." And Winona would, too, although the mere thought of the cannibals guaranteed she would not rest a wink. She had to stay awake to protect Evelyn.

Winona needed to get her hands on a weapon. The Sa-gah-lee, the Great Ones, had taken her rifle and pistols and Evelyn's custom-made small Hawken, and tossed them into a spring the night they were captured. It had surprised her immensely. The Blackfeet, the Crows, the Dakotas, would give anything to own a gun. Stealing one was rated as valiant a deed as stealing a horse or striking an enemy with a coup stick.

During the struggle, Winona had managed to squeeze off a shot. It missed, but Hawk and the others had reacted with shock, as if they had never seen a rifle or pistol or heard one fired. Perhaps that explained why they tossed them in the spring, along with the powder horns and ammo pouches.

There was so much about the Great Ones that was puzzling. Their fear of guns, their primitive clothing—or lack thereof—and primitive weapons. They reminded Winona of the Digger Shoshones who inhabited the country to the south and were considered one of the poorest and weakest of tribes.

The Diggers were so different from her people, the Wind River Shoshones, that Winona found it hard to think of them as being in any way related. Yet their two tongues were similar, and according to stories passed down from the beginning of time, they had once been one big tribe. It later split, and now her people, the Shoshones, lived farther east and had adopted many of the customs of the Plains tribes, while the Diggers, the Shoshokos, still lived much as their ancestors had done at the dawn of the world.

"Ma, can I ask you a question?"

Winona tenderly ran a finger across her daughter's brow. "You are not stalling, are you?" Ever since Evelyn was knee-high to a buffalo calf, she had put off going to sleep as long as possible. She was a master at stalling, at concocting a thousand and one excuses to postpone the inevitable.

"No. I want to know how you abide it?"

"Abide what?"

Evelyn nodded at the Great Ones. "Stuff like this. There's always someone or something out to hurt us. If it isn't hostiles, it's wild animals or a flood or an avalanche. I just don't see how you stand it."

Winona shrugged. "It is part of our life. We must learn to accept the bad with the good, and do all in our power to lessen the dangers."

"How can we when they're all over the place?" Evelyn countered. "Grizzlies and painters are everywhere. Tribes like the Piegans and the Bloods are always out for our scalps." Evelyn bit her lower lip, then said with unaccustomed vehemence, "I hate it. I just hate it."

"I never knew you felt so strongly about this."

Evelyn placed a hand under her head and gazed wistfully at the stars. "I can't wait until I'm old enough to go live in a city. I won't have to worry about being killed when I step out the front door."

"That is why you want to move away?"

"A big part of it. Ever since I was small, Ma, I've always had to be on my guard. Pa and you were always telling me to be on the watch for bears and mountain lions and war parties and such."

"We have to do the same," Winona mentioned. "Everyone does. When your cousins leave their village to go pick berries or find roots, they, too, worry about bears and the like. But they are used to it."

"I'll never be," Evelyn declared, and brightened. "Do you remember that time Pa took us to Kansas City?"

"Yes. We shopped and ate at a restaurant and had a lot of fun."

"I'll say! And do you know what? I never worried once the whole time. No one was trying to kill me. No animals were out to tear me apart. I could walk down the streets and feel safe. That's why I want to go there."

"And not because you despise the Shoshones?"

"What? Where'd you ever get that idea, Ma? How could I not like them? I'm part Shoshone myself."

Winona kissed her daughter's temple. "Do what you feel you must. But I will hardly ever get to see you again."

"Oh, shucks, Ma. Do you think I won't come visit a lot?"

"You and your husband will always be welcome at our cabin."

"Husband?" Evelyn giggled. "I'm never fixing to marry. Boys are too silly and bossy for me."

"Your outlook may change one day." Winona could recall having the same sentiments when she was Evelyn's age.

"I doubt it. Having a husband would be a lot like having a brother. And Zach was always a pain in my backside, as Pa would say."

"That will be enough of that kind of talk," Winona chided.

Yawning, Evelyn closed her eyes and said quietly, "I'm awful hungry, Ma. When will we eat again?"

"Soon, I hope. Tomorrow maybe. I am hungry too."

Winona stroked her daughter's hair and went on doing so until Evelyn's heavy breathing revealed she had succumbed to blissful sleep. Curling up next to her, an arm thrown protectively across Evelyn's back, Winona tried to follow her child's example. But every time she dozed off, another fiendish cry from on high snapped her awake. Toward dawn, when the screams dwindled, she fell into a sleep so deep that she did not realize Hawk was shaking her until an outburst from Evelyn roused her.

"Quit doing that! Can't you see she's resting!"

Befuddled, so drowsy she could barely think, Winona sat up. The eastern sky was aglow; a harbinger of sunrise. "Yes?" she said in the tongue of the Great Ones.

"We go," Hawk directed.

The warriors were getting ready. All the horses had been collected and retied in a string, and the fire had been allowed to burn low.

"How many more days of this?" Winona asked in Shoshone, wishing she could also do it in the Sa-gah-lee tongue. Hawk's forehead furrowed in perplexity until she pointed to the east and arced her arm westward several times to symbolize the passage of the sun through the heavens.

The warrior smiled and pointed at a point in the sky.

"What's that mean?" Evelyn asked.

"It means we will reach their village early this afternoon," Winona said.

"That's great, Ma!"

Was it? Winona wondered. Or were they, as the whites liked to say, going from the frying pan into the fire?

Chapter Four

As the ledge under his right foot crumpled like termite-ridden wood, Nate King did the only thing he could do. He threw himself to the left to get back on firm footing. But in his haste he forgot about the vertical fold in the rock, which jutted outward five or six inches, with the result that his chest bumped against it so hard he was knocked backward.

Nate's arms flailed at empty air and he teetered, about to plunge headlong to the bottom and the jagged boulders waiting to splinter his body to bits. For harrowing heartbeats his life hung in the balance.

Then, heaving forward, Nate pressed against the cliff, clutching it as a drowning man would clutch a floating log. His left foot supported his entire weight; his right was suspended in space. After he had steadied himself, Nate slowly slid his right leg next to his left. With both moccasins on the ledge, he sidled toward where he had originally been. Suddenly noises from above transformed him into marble.

The creatures were back, their grunts mixed with guttural sounds that must be their equivalent of speech. Several stocky shapes appeared, above where the other creature had plunged to its death.

Nate tried to sink into the stone. They were peering straight down and hadn't noticed him yet, but they would if they glanced toward him. Their guttural chatter stopped when they saw the body.

Anticipating the worst, Nate thought for sure one of them would spot him. But they stepped back from view none the wiser. He didn't move for a good fifteen minutes, until he felt confident they were truly gone. Turning, he sank down with his legs over the edge.

Nate had changed his mind. He'd wait until daylight to attempt to reach the top so he could see what he was doing and better gauge the risks.

Like a moth drawn to a flame, his gaze was drawn to the distant campfire once more. It was damned aggravating. All his hard effort to overtake the war party, and now he would have to make up for lost time and overtake them again. His only consolation was that it shouldn't take long. By next sunset, if not sooner.

A grunt from below stiffened him.

Nate looked down, figuring to find the three creatures, but the hairy behemoth that lumbered out of the dense, benighted forest and raised its muzzle to the wind was a monster of a whole new sort. It had four legs, not two, and a pronounced hump on its front shoulders that identified it as the lord of the wild, the undisputed master of all it surveyed, the single most feared animal west of the muddy Mississippi.

A grizzly had caught the scent of blood. Sniffing loudly, it shuffled toward the boulders, its long claws gleaming dully. Rising onto its massive hind legs, it regarded the disjointed heap it was about to eat.

As the bear sank onto all fours, from out of the undergrowth materialized the three beast-men who had been on top of the cliff.

Here was no common sight: a living mountain of sinew, claws, and teeth confronted by semihuman abominations every whit as ferocious and merciless. The most violent of bears pitted against the most untamed of brutes.

Nate assumed the beast-men would speedily retreat into the undergrowth, but to his astonishment they stood their ground and met the bear's resounding roar with fierce roars of their own. The grizzly reared onto its hind legs again to intimidate them, but the tactic had the opposite effect. Hefting their thick spears, the beast-men spread out and advanced, perhaps with the aim of driving the bear off.

It seemed to work. Dropping back down, the bear lumbered to the north. But grizzlies were as unpredictable as they were immense, and this one was no exception. Just when it seemed the bear was about to trot off into the woods, it wheeled and shook the towering peaks with its mightiest roar yet. Then, its mouth wide, its formidable teeth bared, it bore down on the three beast-men like a bull buffalo gone amok.

The trio didn't bolt, didn't flee. Quite the contrary. Howling like banshees, they charged the onrushing titan, the foremost casting his spear when the bear was still twenty feet off. It cleaved the darkness in a blur and sliced into the grizzly near its left shoulder.

Halting, the bear snapped and clawed at the stout shaft but couldn't dislodge it, not until it gripped the spear in its iron jaws and wildly tossed its head. Finally, the spear came out—along with a geyser of blood.

The beast-men closed in, the two who still had spears moving to either side of the griz. Nate had a hunch they'd fought bears before, that their coordinated attack was born of prior experience.

The grizzly turned toward the beast-man on its left.

Immediately, the one on the right hurled his spear with all the power in his husky frame. The bear yowled as the spear bit deep. But this time, instead of uselessly snapping at it, the grizzly barreled toward the man-brute who had thrown it.

The first beast-man had stooped and hoisted a sizable boulder aloft. He let fly with his missile and it struck the bear on the hump, doing no real harm. But it incited the grizzly to a fever pitch of raw rage the likes of which few had ever witnessed.

A sweep of a paw sent an adversary flying. Another battering blow sent a second foe tumbling. That left the brute who had not yet used his spear, but who did so now, slicing it deep into the bear's side.

The grizzly now had two spears jutting from its body, yet it didn't fall. The beast-man who had just speared it went down under a smashing paw and the bear's head dipped as it went to sink its teeth into the beast-man's leg. In a surprising move, the two-legged brute wrapped his corded arms around the bear's neck and attempted to do the impossible: to strangle a grizzly alive.

His companions flew to his aid, one beating at the bear with a rock, the other striving to wrest a spear out to use it again.

The outcome, though, was never in doubt. No matter how strong or how determined they were, the beast-men could not long withstand the living embodiment of animal savagery. By dint of size and strength and the size of its teeth and claws, the bear would soon rip them to bloody pieces.

Then a new element intruded. Four more creatures streamed from the firs and without hesitation leaped into the fray, thrusting their spears into the grizzly again and again while simultaneously attempting to avoid its raking claws.

Bruin and beast-men were a continuous whirl of motion—spinning, springing, slashing, striking. The man-brutes were repeatedly sent tumbling, only to vault erect and hurl themselves anew into the midst of the bedlam.

What with the dark and the confusion, Nate couldn't tell which side was getting the worst of it. Although woefully outnumbered and severely wounded, the grizzly was more than holding its own.

The next moment one of the beast-men broke from the battle, scrambled up onto a boulder bigger than the bear, and raised his spear high above his head in both hands. As if on cue, the others engaged in a concerted onslaught, driving the bear back against the boulder their companion was on.

Arcing into the air, the man-brute alighted on the grizzly's broad back. Instantly, he sheared his spear into its unprotected flesh, sinking it deep, so deep that when he endeavored to yank it out, it wouldn't budge.

A roar to end all roars, a thunderous, slavering roar of commingled fury and pain, reverberated off the cliff. The grizzly reared onto its hind legs one last time, pitching the man-beast on its back to the dirt. The others darted in, lancing their spears into its vulnerable belly, but the real harm had already been done, the death stroke had already been delivered. The grizzly took a few halting, stumbling steps, its paws swinging almost lazily, then it keeled forward, toppling like a redwood, and crashed to earth. A cloud of dust rose around it, and when the dust settled the lord of the mountains was as still as the boulders.

Defying all logic, the beast-men had beaten it.

Shoshones would have whooped and hollered, celebrating their victory. But the creatures turned from their conquest as if their monumental feat were of no importance.

All were bleeding, some were limping, and one brute's arm hung at an unnatural angle. Collecting their spears, they clustered around the one who had fallen off the cliff, ringing his broken body, and squatted.

Nate took it for granted that they were showing respect for a fallen comrade. They were demonstrating more intelligence and compassion that he had thought possible. Then the unspeakable occurred.

One of the bigger beast-men gripped the dead brute's arm, lifted it to his mouth, and took a bite. It was the cue for the rest to partake. Bending low, they sank their fangs into the body with relish, growling and tearing at it like a pack of ravenous coyotes.

Nate's gut churned. They were eating their own kind! And if they would do that, they would assuredly eat him or anyone else they caught. His original opinion of them had been right. They were less than human and worse than vile. They were the most repulsive of two-legged creatures known; they were cannibals.

They were literally tearing the dead one apart, ripping off large grisly chunks with their teeth and fingers, chunks they enthusiastically stuffed into their blood-flecked mouths and then chewed with obnoxious delight.

Nate couldn't stand to watch, but he couldn't bring himself to look away. He saw one of them worrying the throat, saw another lean over the groin. Bitter bile rose in his throat, and he forced it down.

Taking his spear, a cannibal opened the chest cavity. Shoving his hands into the body, he groped about, then pulled out the heart and held it aloft as if it were a trophy. A trophy he greedily crammed into his mouth.

Repulsed beyond measure, Nate gazed toward the war party's campfire. His stomach churned worse as he realized the true degree of danger Winona and Evelyn were in. If the cannibals attacked and overwhelmed the war party, his wife and daughter would be *eaten*. He had to get to them, had to get out of there. Twisting, he looked up at the top of the cliff.

Dirt and a few pebbles rattled down off the ledge. Freezing in place, Nate glanced down at the cannibals. One shifted and scanned the cliff, seeking the source of the noise. It was chewing lustily on part of an arm or a leg.

Nate tensed for an outcry, but there was none. The creature didn't spy him. After a bit it turned back to the others, all of them chomping and grunting and snorting like hogs at a feed trough.

For the time being, Nate wasn't going anywhere. He resigned himself to waiting until the cannibals were done feasting, but he never counted on them taking as long as they did. Half an hour went by. An hour. Two hours. They were in no hurry. Not when they enjoyed gorging themselves at the expense of one of their own.

At one point a dispute arose.

Nate had leaned back and was recollecting the time he and a friend of his, another mountain man by the name of Scott Kendall, took their families up into a high country park for a week of rest and relaxation. They had fished and played and had so much fun that none of them wanted to leave.

A growl below ended his reverie. Two of the cannibals were fighting over a morsel. One tried to grab it from the other and was pushed onto his haunches. Both rose, snarling menacingly, and for a while it appeared they would tear into one another. But it was all bluster, like two lynx snarling at each other over a deer carcass. They growled and stamped and shook their knobby fists, and then the one that started it abruptly sat back down and chose another piece.

Nate wished they had fought, wished they had killed each other so there would be two fewer cannibals to contend with later.

Another hour dragged by at a turtle's pace. Nate caught himself grinding his teeth in frustration. At the rate they were going about it, they would take all night.

Sure enough, that was exactly what they did.

It wasn't until the faintest of glows marked the sky to the east that the cannibals rose and moved off. Some were contentedly rubbing their bellies. Others were licking their fingers. One picked at his teeth with a sliver of bone.

Ironically, the grizzly lay untouched. Bear meat was delicious, and it was highly sought after by whites and red men alike. But the cannibals had no interest in it. They would rather eat another person than a wild animal.

Nate had seldom been so revolted. Whether it was the cannibalism, the creatures themselves, or an instinct born of humankind's dark and mysterious past, he loathed them with a passion bordering on pure hatred. They were despicable, aberrations of Nature, a travesty of all that was human. Were it in his power, he would wipe them off the face of the earth.

Now and then Nate caught glimpses of them as they hiked northward through the forest. When they disappeared over a rise he slowly rose and faced the cliff. Spurred by his desire to reach Winona and Evelyn as quickly as possible, he raised his arms as high as they would go, cautiously bent at the knees, girded himself, and leaped straight up.

Nate missed his hold. His fingers hooked the rim, but it was loosely packed dirt, not solid rock. Grasping it was like trying to clutch grains of sand, and before he could firm his grip his fingers slipped and he dropped back down onto the ledge. Or, rather, onto the edge of the ledge. His left foot lost its purchase and he canted backward. He tried to regain his balance, but the act of pumping his left leg upward caused his other foot to slide off.

Nate fell. In desperation he flung himself at the ledge, slamming his forearms onto it and arresting his plunge. His legs, swinging wildly, smashed against the wall, causing him to almost lose his newly regained hold. His pulse racing, he clung on for all he was worth.

The strain on his arms and shoulders was tremendous. Nate attempted to lever himself up but couldn't raise himself high enough to throw his leg onto the ledge. After the third attempt he desisted and hung there, catching his breath.

The sky was brightening fast. Enough for Nate to see hairline cracks under his forearms. Remembering how unstable the ledge was, he slowly wriggled to the left until he was past them.

Nate couldn't hang there forever. Sooner or later he would tire. He had to get up on the ledge while he still could.

Jamming his elbows against the wall, Nate began to swing his body from side to side. Only a little bit at first, then wider and wider in a steady rhythm, until, at the apex of a swing to the left, he threw his foot onto the ledge. Now that he had added leverage, he pulled himself up inch by painstaking inch. His shoulders protested, but soon he had both legs on the ledge and he lay there gasping for breath and waiting for the hammering in his chest to go away.

It had been close. Much too close.

Nate faced eastward. A new day had been born, and the golden crown of the sun was spreading its radiance across the earth. He was glad to be alive to see it. In the forest birds were astir and somewhere an early rising squirrel was chattering in irritation.

The glow from the campfire was gone. Nate had a rough idea of where the camp had been, but although he scoured the general vicinity, he saw no trace of anyone.

When his shoulders stopped hurting, Nate sat up and examined the rock surface above. There were no handholds, just as he had thought. His only recourse was to jump for it and pray that this time he didn't slip.

Twisting, Nate eased upward. As he rose he noticed a depression in the rock about half a foot above the ledge. It was roughly circular and about the size of an apple. Too low to be a handhold, it would make an excellent foothold.

Nate wedged the toe of his right moccasin into the hole. Raising his arms, he concentrated on the rim. Concentrated as he tucked at the knees, concentrated as he gauged the distance, concentrated on the rim and nothing else as he sprang upward. His hands hooked the brim, and like before, the loose dirt threatened to prove his undoing. But this time he thrust even higher, thanks to the foothold, giving himself an added boost, just enough to prop his arms on the brim of the cliff as he had done on the ledge.

In a smooth motion Nate powered himself up and over. Wasting no more time, he stood and sprinted toward a slope that would take him lower down the mountain. He looked for his pistol along the way but didn't spot it, and he wasn't about to spend half an hour searching. All he cared about was reaching Winona and Evelyn.

Fatigue nipped at Nate's mind, hunger gnawed at his stomach. He ignored both. He was scraped and bruised, but he ignored that, too. Jogging with the tireless stamina of a frontiersman bred to hardship and toil, he didn't stop until two hours later when he reached the bottom. And then he only rested for a few minutes.

The war party's camp was another quarter of a mile to the south. On the off chance the warriors were still there, Nate proceeded slowly, availing himself of all available cover. He was several hundreds yards out when he saw a circle of trampled grass with a pile of charred wood in the center.

They were gone.

Nate warily moved into the open, his hands on the Bowie and tomahawk. Finding where Winona and Evelyn had been lying took only a few moments. Squatting, he placed his left hand on the exact spot, his yearning to be with them again so acute, his chest hurt.

Turning to the embers, Nate poked through them. Only a few were still warm. As he had suspected, the warriors had lit out to the southwest at dawn, or thereabouts. He was three, maybe three and a half hours behind them.

As Nate rose and resumed jogging his stomach began to cramp. He moved more slowly than he had before. Not by choice, but because his body had been pushed to near the limit of its exceptional endurance and if he didn't go easy he risked collapsing from exhaustion.

As the sun climbed, so did the temperature. It was another hot, sultry summer's day, and Nate was sweating profusely before another half an hour elapsed.

The warriors were wending steadily into the mountains, climbing progressively higher as they went. Their footprints showed they were moving at a brisker pace than they had so far, which Nate construed as a clue that they were nearing their destination.

Presently the tracks intersected a well-worn trail, bearing west. It saw regular use. Nate discovered tracks of men, women, and children. So a village *was* close by. The only hoofprints were those of the animals being led by the war party, a clear sign that the tribe did not possess horses of their own.

The sun was almost at its zenith when Nate came to a bend between forested slopes. Fatigued to the bone, he moved into a stand of aspens a dozen yards to the south to rest for a short while. No more than fifteen, twenty minutes at the most, and he would go on. Wearily sinking onto his back, he let out a long sigh. His stomach rumbled, reminding him again of how hungry he was.

From his possibles bag Nate took the second-to-last piece of pemmican. He had been saving them to eat as a last resort if he couldn't find any other food, but he needed to boost his energy and strength. Taking a bite, he winced as his mouth puckered as if he had bitten into a lemon. He had gone so long without a bite to eat that his taste buds had recoiled.

Chewing slowly, Nate closed his eyes. He was tired, so very, very tired. If he fell asleep, he wouldn't wake up until the next day. And he couldn't permit that to happen. Winona and Evelyn needed him; he would be damned if he would let them down.

A feeling of utter lethargy filled his limbs. Nate resisted, but feebly, his willpower a shadow of what it normally was. He stopped chewing as a fuzzy warm sensation enveloped him, a sensation of sinking into the biggest and softest pillow in the world. All he had to do was let his consciousness go, relinquish control, and he would experience the unfettered bliss of undisturbed slumber.

Nate began to sink deeper into the fuzziness. He heard children laughing and women talking in a language he didn't understand. A dream, he thought, and it snapped him awake. *I must not fall asleep.* Sitting up, he shook his head to dispel lingering cobwebs and didn't quite succeed. He still heard the laughter and female voices. Then he realized they were real, and glanced toward the trail.

Four women were seated in the shade of a pine near the bend. With them were four children varying in ages from about eight to fourteen. The women had large baskets brimming with roots and plants that they had apparently spent most of the morning gathering. Now they were on their way back to their village.

The whole bunch was jabbering happily, acting as if they didn't have a care in the world. No one would guess the countryside swarmed with cannibals. Or did it? Nate had begun to suspect the cannibals were nocturnal, that for whatever reason they seldom if ever were abroad during the day.

The women were the same size as the warriors, which was to say short of stature and slender of build. They had the same oval faces and high cheekbones, the same almond eyes and inky hair. Their dresses were made of rabbit fur, not buckskin, and stitched together as crudely as the moccasins of the men.

The children, two boys and two girls, were like children everywhere—giggling and squealing and not able to sit still for one second. The boys started chasing the girls around and around the women, who chatted on undisturbed.

Suddenly one of the girls broke away, dashed across the trail, and ran toward the aspens with one of the boys hard on her heels.

Automatically Nate flattened, his right hand flicking to the Bowie. But he just as quickly jerked his hand away. Under no circumstances would he harm a couple of children.

The young girl was almost to the stand. A shout from one of the women stopped her as she was about to burst in among them. Rotating, she laughed at the boy, mocking him, then angled to the right, eluding his outstretched hand. He laughed, too, and chased after her as she looped back toward the rest.

Nate raised his head. The women were standing, their baskets under their arms. Two by two they ambled on past the bend, their children gamboling like frisky otters.

Giving them a minute's lead, Nate pushed upright and glided along the trail until he could see what lay on the other side of the mountain. Before his gaze unfolded a narrow valley, half a mile long and half that wide, covered with grass. There had been trees at one time, as scores and scores of old stumps testified, but they had been chopped down, every last one, and no others had been allowed to grow. High mountains bordered the valley to the north and south, natural barriers contributing to its isolation.

At the west end reared a mesa three hundred feet high, its sides as sheer as the cliff Nate had been trapped on. Gaining the summit appeared to be impossible, yet there were people up there. Moving figures and tendrils of smoke pegged it as the location of the long-sought village.

The dirt trail broadened, becoming as wide as a road. A heavily traveled road. The women and children were not the only ones using it. Others were moving toward the mesa or coming from it.

Nate scowled. He couldn't possibly cross the valley in broad daylight. The tribe had seen to that by clearing it of trees and undergrowth. A precaution against surprise attack, he reckoned.

Backing away, Nate pivoted and headed around the bend toward the aspens. He'd spend the rest of the day there and sneak to the mesa after dark. There had to be a way to the top, and he would find it.

A sharp exclamation stopped him cold.

Glancing ahead, Nate saw three warriors who were every bit as surprised as he was. But they didn't stay surprised for long. Strident yells rang out as they raised their weapons and attacked.

Chapter Five

"Why do they always smile when they see us, Ma?"

Winona King was as puzzled as her daughter. "I do not know, Blue Flower," she answered. They were nearing the west end of the grassy valley and had passed over a dozen Sa-gah-lee on the dirt road, all of whom stopped to stare and smile as if they were long-lost relatives instead of captives.

"Maybe they're not as bad as we think," Evelyn commented. "Maybe they're fixing to adopt us into the tribe like the Blackfeet did that time with Zach."

"Maybe," Winona said. It would be preferable to death, but it would leave her with the dilemma of what to do if a warrior took her as his wife. She would never be unfaithful to Nate, never let any man be intimate with her no matter what the consequences.

Evelyn gazed at the mesa, towering to the clouds before them. "It's going to take forever to climb."

Winona bent her head back. A couple of warriors were silhouetted against the sky. Sentries, she reckoned.

Tapping Hawk on the back, she pointed at the crest and asked, "Village there?"

"Yes," the leader said, adding information Winona only caught snatches of. Something about a warrior who had found the mesa long ago.

"I don't see a trail leading up," Evelyn remarked. "How do they expect us to get up there? Sprout wings and fly?"

Winona did not see a way up either. The sides were as sheer as marble. It was too high to use rope, too high, even, for handholds. Most people would tire long before reaching the rim. Again she tapped Hawk, pointed, and said, "How?"

Grinning, the warrior nodded at large boulders dotting the bottom of the escarpment. "Wait," he said.

The mystery was explained a minute later. An opening appeared, an opening the boulders concealed until a person was right on top of it.

"Hey, what's that?" Evelyn said.

"A tunnel" was Winona's guess, eroded out of the rock over many eons by water seeping from above. Guards weren't posted at the entrance, which surprised her. A pile of broken tree limbs lay to the right of it, a pile of grass to the left.

Hawk brought the war party to a halt. At his order, Stone wrapped some of the grass around the end of one of the branches and lit the makeshift torch using two pieces of quartz he carried in a small pouch stashed under his breechclout. All the warriors carried near-identical pouches. It was how they kindled their campfires. Winona had observed that they treated the quartz with reverence, as if it were of great value. And to them, perhaps it was. In the Rockies quartz was everywhere, but Winona had not seen sign of any since well before she was taken captive.

Stone gave the torch to Hawk, who motioned for Winona to stay close to him. The walls were caked with the dust, and there was a musty scent.

"It's nice in here, Ma," Evelyn said.

That it was, Winona agreed. Compared to the stifling heat outside, the tunnel was wonderfully cool, almost invigorating.

They had gone only a dozen yards when Winona saw five or six women approaching in single file from the other direction. They greeted Hawk warmly, with reverence, and he made a comment that provoked laughter.

The tunnel floor began angling upward by gradual degrees. When Winona took her next stride she bumped her toe. Glancing down, she saw the edge of a step, one of many, a whole flight carved from the solid stone. The tunnel, then, was the handiwork of man, not Nature.

"Are these what I think they are?" Evelyn said.

"Stairs," Winona confirmed.

"Did the Great Ones make them?"

Winona said Hawk's name. When he turned, she said, "Sa-gah-lee?" and bent to run her hand over the steps.

"No," Hawk replied. He did not elaborate.

The tunnel was wide enough for four people to walk abreast and twice as high as Winona. More than big enough for the horses. The clatter of their hooves pealed like echoes in a canyon.

As Winona's gaze roved over the walls she spied splashes of color. Curious, she swiped at the dust and was amazed to discover finely detailed paintings. Artistic renderings of people and animals, some of which she recognized, some of which were outlandish.

"Hawk?" she said. "Sa-gah-lee?"

"Old Ones," he said.

Evelyn was as fascinated as Winona. "Look at them all!" she exclaimed. "That one there is a man with a bow, but what's that critter next to him? The thing with the horns growing out the front of its head?"

Winona could only shrug. The creature was depicted as being much larger than the man. It had a shaggy coat and two great curved horns, one either side of its mouth. It also had a second tail right above the horns. Totally preposterous, she thought. Then she recalled a conversation she had once had with Nate. He owned a collection of books, and among them was a volume on foreign lands. "Do you remember your father telling us about a place called Africa?"

"Sure. Where they have lions with manes and lots of monkeys and big hogs they call hippos." Evelyn lit up like a candle. "And elephants! Big critters with tusks and a nose like a snake!" They had passed the painting, and she glanced back at it. "That was a hairy elephant, wasn't it?"

"I think so, yes."

"Does that mean whoever drew it came all the way here from Africa?"

"I doubt that very much," Winona said. As far-fetched as it seemed, the more logical explanation was that at one time hairy elephants were found in that region. It brought to mind ancient Shoshone legends of a time when giant creatures roamed the land.

Many more paintings adorned the tunnel walls. There were great cats with upper teeth that hung past their lower jaws. Small horselike animals that traveled in herds. A giant bear with a huge, thick tail that was shown on its hind legs, munching leaves. Buffalo, too, but different from those Winona was accustomed to, with much broader heads, longer legs, and horns as wide as her cabin.

There were more. Wolfish creatures with long muzzles, deer with knobs instead of antlers. Other deer with long necks as high as trees, and animals similar to deer but with two humps on their backs.

One of the largest paintings was of an animal as large

as the elephant, only it had a blunt, squarish head with a pair of forked horns above its nostrils.

"What on earth is that one?" Evelyn asked.

"Your guess is as good as mine."

Hawk seemed amused by their reaction. Presently he stopped and held the torch close to the right-hand wall.

A ceremony of some kind was portrayed. Under a full moon dozens of people ringed a man in a headdress who stood over a person lying down. In the man's hand was a knife or dagger, and from it dripped tiny red drops. Drops of blood, Winona realized, and was deeply disturbed when Hawk touched the figure in the headdress, touched the person lying at the man's feet, and pointed at her.

Evelyn gasped. "What's he saying? Do they aim to kill you?"

Winona hoped not. "It could mean anything," she hedged so as not to alarm her.

The next painting was one of the oddest. A huge blazing sun was at the center, and under it dozens of figures lay sprawled on the ground. In the sky were lots of winged shapes. Birds, Winona gathered. The exact kind eluded her.

A few more steps brought them to a painting of skeletons lying under another huge, blazing sun.

"Did all the people die, Ma?"

"Not all of them."

"What makes you say that?"

"Someone survived to paint these scenes."

The tunnel curved sharply upward. From then on the walls were bare. Soon a circle of light foretold an end to their climb.

Twice more they passed Sah-gah-lee coming the other way. In each case, the Great Ones stopped and smiled when they saw Winona and Evelyn. Winona did not know what to make of it.

They emerged into the bright glare of the afternoon

sun. Squinting, Winona saw that the tunnel came out about two hundred yards from the east end of the mesa. Piles of limbs and grass were at this end, too. So was a pile of logs and four guards.

To the west was an incredible sight, a high wall constructed from massive blocks of stone. Beyond were buildings several stories higher than the wall. It was a city, a magnificent city. At its center reared a tower crowned by a glittery sphere with a polished surface a lot like glass.

A wide gate admitted them into a maze of narrow streets. As Winona passed through the portal she was shocked to see that her initial impression had been wrong. It wasn't a magnificent city at all. It was a decrepit, crumbling city, millennia past its prime, a city on the verge of devastation.

The stone blocks were not really stone at all. They were made of baked earth or clay that reminded Winona of adobe. Most were badly weathered with age. Many were cracked or split wide. Originally the blocks had been neatly aligned, but now the majority tilted one way or another, knocked askew by a geologic upheaval in a bygone era.

Everything was in dire disrepair. Walls bulged outward or inward. Whole sections lay in shattered ruin. Buildings canted on the verge of collapse. It was a dead domain unfit for human habitation.

Winona couldn't understand why the Great Ones lived there. It wouldn't take much to bring the whole city crashing down around their ears. They would be better off in the valley.

The farther into the city they traveled, the more Sagah-lee they encountered. Always, it was the same. The men and women took one look and broke into warm smiles.

Winona's unease grew. So, apparently, did Evelyn's. Winona felt her small fingers slip into her palm, and she squeezed them to reassure her. "Everything will be all right."

"Will it? I'm a big girl now, remember? You can be honest with me."

"I always am," Winona said, and inwardly winced at her fib. To spare her daughter she would bend the truth if need be.

Before them loomed the tower. Situated in the middle of a broad public square, it was in the same awful condition as everything else. One crack, in particular, ran from the ground to the glassy sphere.

Hawk led Winona and Evelyn to a platform in the tower's shadow. A short flight of rickety wooden stairs brought them to the top, where a long stone slab sprinkled with red stains gave Winona pause.

Word of their arrival was spreading like a prairie fire and Great Ones were converging from every which way. Men, women, couples, families, they packed into the square. Whenever new arrivals beheld Winona, they grinned and happily clapped one another on the back as if she were long-lost kin miraculously restored.

Seventy or eighty Great Ones were present when Hawk raised his arms to silence the murmur and launched into a speech. He addressed them much too rapidly for Winona to fathom much of what he said.

Everyone was staring at her. Or so it felt. Uncomfortable under their close scrutiny, Winona repeatedly shifted from one foot to the other. Evelyn was glued to her leg, as scared as a rabbit in a forest crawling with coyotes.

Gazing out over the assemblage, Winona noticed a few listeners who were plainly not Sa-gah-lee, two women and a man. The former were Flatheads by the look of them, sisters, maybe, in their twenties, wearing buckskin dresses. The latter was an old white man with white hair and wrinkled features, his spare frame clothed in a tattered buckskin shirt and a breechclout.

He hardly ever looked up and his mouth was forever moving, as if he were perpetually muttering to himself.

"More captives!" Evelyn whispered, pointing at the Flatheads. "That must mean the Great Ones won't make wolf meat of us after all."

On the one hand, Winona was encouraged; on the other, it increased the likelihood a warrior would take her as his wife. Suddenly strong hands gripped on her arms, and she jumped as if pricked by a pin.

Stone, Antelope, Growing Grass, and Runs Slow had silently come up behind her. Stone pinned her arms while Antelope, holding a short length of rope, hunkered.

"What—?" Winona blurted in Shoshone.

Antelope looped the rope around her left ankle. Divining its purpose, Winona went to resist. Growing Grass hindered her by stooping and wrapping his arms around her lower legs as Runs Slow pried Evelyn off.

Hawk stopped in the middle of a sentence and glanced at them. "Do not resist," he commanded.

Winona resented being hobbled like a horse, but what could she do, outnumbered as she was? Swallowing her pride, she meekly nodded.

Evelyn, though, struggled in Runs Slow's grip. "Let go of me, darn you!" she fumed. "And let go of my ma!"

"Do not raise a fuss," Winona said, in the hope they wouldn't hobble Evelyn if she behaved.

Evelyn paid no heed. "I said let go!" she repeated, and kicked Runs Slow in the shin. Squawking, he released her, and she leaped at Stone like a berserk bobcat, raking a cheek with her nails.

Winona saw Stone cock an arm to backhand her and lunged, grabbing Evelyn before anyone else could. "Enough!" she cried.

"You can't let them tie you!" Evelyn wailed, resisting

70

as strenuously as she had resisted Runs Slow. "We'll never get away!"

"Behave!" Winona shouted, and did something she rarely did with her children: She employed physical force, shaking Evelyn by the shoulders none too gently. "You are only making it worse!"

Stunned, Evelyn went limp. "Ma, you hurt me!"

"I am sorry," Winona said sincerely.

Shoshones rarely punished their children, and when they did, they never beat them or smacked them or in any manner physically abused them. The Shoshones believed it broke a child's spirit. Boys would lose the independence of mind that made them worthy warriors, and women would become too timid to be useful wives. It had astounded Winona no end when Nate informed her that whites routinely spanked their children, that, in fact, his own father had beaten him more times than he could count with a thick stick or a belt, leaving welts that took days or weeks to heal. Yet Nate had grown into a hardy man of indomitable will and courage.

Stone finished hobbling her and stood. Winona thought he was done, but Growing Grass handed him another short length of rope and Stone squatted next to Evelyn. Winona looked in mute appeal at Hawk.

"It must be," the leader said.

"Ma?" Evelyn said apprehensively as the hobble was applied. "We've got to do something!"

"Stay calm."

"How can I?" Fright filled Evelyn's eyes, and she was poised like a fawn for flight. "How can *you*?"

"Listen to me," Winona said, bending so they were eye-to-eye. "I hate this as much as you do. But if we fight back they might do worse. They might lock us in a room and keep us under guard every hour of the day. For now we must go along with them. But I promise you I have not given up. When the right time comes, we will escape."

71

Evelyn calmed considerably. "All right. I'll do as you say. I just hope we don't have to wait long before our chance comes."

"You and I both."

Hawk turned to the crowd and spoke at length. When he was done, he said to Winona, "Follow me."

The hobbles made walking a chore. They had to swing their legs outward to take a step, but not swing them too far or they would be thrown off balance. Winona descended the short stairs first in case Evelyn fell so she could catch her.

Hawk and Stone were waiting. So were twenty or thirty Great Ones who trailed along as Winona and Evelyn were ushered down one narrow street after another. They passed a building in a shambles and halted in front of a single-story dwelling in fair condition. Like most, the entrance lacked a door, but the windows were covered with deer hides.

The two Flatheads and the white man were among those who had followed. Hawk beckoned, and the sisters hurried forward. The white man, though, did not move until Hawk called out, "One-Eye, you too!"

Muttering under his breath, the spindly, gray-haired figure joined them. His face was seamed with more wrinkles than most ten people. Blue veins laced his skinny arms and knobby legs. His ragged beard had not been combed in years. He refused to look up until Hawk told him to, and when he did, Winona saw he had a thick ridge of scar tissue where his left eye had been. His other eye was brown, wide, and vaguely unfocused.

Hawk barked at the three. The Flatheads both answered, "Yes." But One-Eye was gazing at the ground again, his lips moving soundlessly. Only after Hawk poked him did he acknowledge he had heard by brusquely nodding.

Frowning, Hawk departed, and the rest of the Great Ones dispersed.

Not a single warrior stayed to watch over them. Winona and the others had been left on their own. "I told you our chance would come," she whispered to Evelyn.

The white man's head jerked up. "English? You spoke English, by God!" Seizing Winona by the shoulders, he studied her face, his good eye boring into her with relentless intensity. "But you're not white!"

"I am Shoshone," Winona calmly answered. "And I do not like being manhandled." She shrugged free.

The man's good eye jerked from side to side in agitation. "How is it you know the white tongue so well?"

"My husband is white. I am Winona King. Who are you?"

The question seemed to startle him. "Who am I?" the man repeated, and tittered. "How long has it been since I said my real name? Ten years? Twenty?" He tittered louder, spittle dribbling down over his thin lower lip onto his beard.

Winona held Evelyn close, concerned the man was not quite right in the head.

"Ezriah Hampton, at your service, ma'am," he said, and gave a courtly bow, chortling as he did. "Formerly of the glorious state of Delaware, but for the past couple of decades a resident of the lost city of the long dead Elders."

"I am pleased to make your acquaintance, Ezriah Hampton," Winona said.

Ezriah uncoiled and grinned lopsidedly. Most of his upper teeth were gone, and the teeth he had left were yellow. "Did you hear that? She called me by my name. Sweeter music was never heard. I am in your debt, lady. But say the word, and I'll topple yon ramparts for you."

Evelyn tugged on Winona's dress and whispered louder than she should, "Is he addlepated, Ma?"

"Addlepated!" Ezriah practically roared. "That's a

73

fine thing to say to a coon who has endured all I have!"
He cackled, his good eye jerking nonstop now. "But you
know, dearie, you could well be right. I haven't been
myself in more years than I can remember. So if you
see part of me wandering around, tell it to come find
me, will you?" Snickering, he walked into the building.

"He scares me, Ma," Evelyn said.

Winona looked at the sisters, who stood shyly to one
side. She had friends among the Flatheads, and at the
annual trapper rendezvous had spent many an hour
visiting them. "I am Winona, a Shoshone," she intro-
duced herself in their tongue. "This is my daughter,
Blue Flower. I know you are Flatheads, friends of my
people. My heart is happy to meet you."

Both women beamed and excitedly started talking at
the same time. Catching themselves, they giggled nervously, and the taller of the two said, "We are happy
to meet you, as well. I am Spotted Doe. My younger
sister is Eagle Shadow."

"How long have you been here?"

"One moon," Spotted Doe said. "We were taken
when we were gathering berries near our village." Sorrow gripped her, and she grew downcast. "We miss our
families, our husbands. We thought they would come
for us, but no one ever did. Now our fate cannot be
avoided."

"We are masters of own fate," Winona amended,
thinking Spotted Doe referred to being held captive.

Spotted Doe's sorrow deepened. "We thought as you
do, once. But we have tried to get away and always
been caught."

Winona gestured at the doorway. "What about him?"

"The crazy one? He is useless. He refused to help us,
and he mocked us when we were brought back."

"I want to talk to him," Winona said, and went in.
The hides over the windows mired the interior in
gloom. They had been tied to poles attached to the up-

74

per frame, so all she had to do to admit more light was slide them to one side.

"Don't do that. I like it dark." Ezriah Hampton was hunkered in a corner, his broomstick forearms across his bony knee.

Dust sparkled in beams of sunlight as Winona crossed the room. Except for several old mats scattered at random, there were no furnishings. "We need to talk, Ezriah."

The old man smirked. "That's what they all say, dearie. They always want to talk my ears off when they first arrive. But once I answer all their questions, they hardly say another word until the end comes."

Winona sank down in front of him, Evelyn clinging to her left arm. "Did I understand you correctly? You have been here twenty years?"

Ezriah's eye fixed on her, his eyelid twitching spasmodically. "Thereabouts. I don't keep track anymore. What's the use?"

"In all that time the Great Ones have treated you decently?"

"Great Ones?" Ezriah laughed heartily. "A better name for the Sa-gah-lee would be Stupid Ones. They barely eke out a living. This city isn't even theirs. It was built by the Elders. The Sa-gah-lee took it over because it's easy to defend."

"What will they do with my daughter and me?" Winona asked.

"The same thing they do with all the other folks they steal." Ezriah's eye glittered with amusement. "Trust me. You and your sprout won't like it one bit."

"Can you be a little more specific?"

"Ain't she a peach! She wants all the gory details!" Slapping his leg in glee, Ezriah rocked back and forth. "Haven't you heard? Ignorance is bliss. But if you really and truly want your bliss spoiled, I can oblige you."

"Oblige me," Winona goaded.

Ezriah sobered, his wide eye darting to Evelyn and back to Winona again. "Suit yourself, lady. The Great Ones brought you here for the same reason they bring everyone." He paused. "They intend to offer you up at the next full moon."

"Offer us to who?"

"Why, the cannibals, of course. So they can eat you alive."

Chapter Six

As the three warriors bore down on him, Nate King drew his tomahawk and knife. Two held lances and were not quite close enough to use them. But the third man had a bow and already had an arrow nocked. He let fly without taking aim.

The shaft whizzed past Nate's shoulder, convincing him it was certain death to meet their charge in the open. Spinning to his left, he sped toward the woods, and cover. The trio veered to intercept them, but Nate gained the undergrowth well ahead of them. An arrow thudded into a tree as he flew by, prompting him to tuck at the waist and dash into a cluster of saplings. On the other side was a small clearing, which he covered in long bounds.

Tall firs dappled Nate with shadows as he glanced over a shoulder. The warriors had just reached the clearing and were looking about in confusion. They had lost sight of him, but not for long. The one in the middle pointed, and all three leaped in pursuit like wolves after a fleeing elk. They didn't whoop or holler as warriors from most tribes were wont to do. Grimly earnest, they spread out, the archer in the center, an arrow notched and another in his mouth ready for swift use.

A fallen tree barred Nate's path. Running to the left to go around, he nearly pitched into a wide hole that had been created when the tree toppled, wrenching its own roots out of the earth. Jumping down, he hunkered.

The warriors were coming on fast. They had lost sight of him again, and on reaching the fallen tree they stopped. The man farthest from Nate climbed up onto it to scour the forest.

Nate thought for sure they would search for tracks and find him in no time. But the man on the tree hopped down and the trio sprinted around the far end. Fanning out again, they soon blended into the brush and were gone.

Nate didn't linger. Pumping up out of the hole, he retraced his steps to the road, crossed it, and concealed himself in the same stand of aspens he had hid in earlier. Flat on his belly, he rested his chin on his arms.

About twenty minutes later the three warriors reappeared. Disgruntled by their failure, they argued awhile, then headed toward the mesa.

It was entirely possible, Nate reflected, that they would come back with a large search party. Deciding to change position, he moved out of the aspens and into a patch of high weeds. From his new vantage point he could see clear across the valley. Making himself comfortable, he resigned himself to waiting until sunset.

Over an hour went by. Indians came and went, including a hunting party with a buck strung on a pole and another group of women carrying baskets laden with roots and plants. As with most tribes, food-gathering was their uppermost priority. It had to be.

With so many mouths to feed, staving off starvation was a never-ending task.

Nate sat up, his eyes narrowing. A sizable body of men was flowing out from the bottom of the mesa. Turning, he crept off through the weeds and partway up the adjacent slope. In the shelter of a thicket he sat and watched as the threesome who had been after him before returned with eleven companions. At the bend they split into two groups and stalked into the woods on the other side of the road.

Nate grinned to himself. It hadn't occurred to them he had backtracked. By Shoshone standards they were woefully inept.

Most Easterners assumed all Indians were seasoned hunters and trackers, that their wilderness savvy was second to none. But the simple truth was, some tribes were more proficient at woodcraft than others. Just as some were better at warfare and every other aspect of tribal life.

Mountain men loved to debate which tribes excelled the most. The general consensus was that the Apaches were not only the fiercest warriors, they were also some of the best trackers. The Comanches had a reputation for being supremely skilled horsemen, although the Sioux were highly regarded in that respect, also. The Pawnees were noted for their cleverness. Cheyenne women were renowned for their chastity, Crow men for being exceptionally handsome. The tribes that made up the Blackfoot Confederacy were famed for their steadfast hatred of all whites. Utes were wonderful hunters; the Nez Percé were sought after for the marvelous Appaloosas they raised.

As for Nate's adopted people, the Shoshones, they were widely regarded as one of the friendliest tribes anywhere, if not *the* friendliest. Their lodges were always open to whites, and they were one of the few tribes who could rightfully claim they had never slain a white-eye.

Nate liked the Shoshones for a variety of reasons. They were honest, earthy people who could fight when pressed but were not as warlike as the Sioux and the Blackfeet. They devoted as much time to the rearing of their children and the upkeep of their lodges as they did to everything else. If given their druthers, the Shoshones would rather be left alone to live in peace.

Voices alerted Nate to the arrival of a dozen more warriors, reinforcements to assist in the search. He figured they would limit their efforts to the other side of the road, as the first bunch had done, but they paired off and commenced to comb the south side. One pair came straight toward the thicket.

Caught flat-footed, Nate hugged the earth and crabbed backward until he had gone far enough to ensure they wouldn't spot him. A gully enabled him to circle around toward the valley and outflank them.

The sun was on its downward arc. All Nate had to do was outwit the warriors until sunset and he would be safe. Or would he? Nighttime was when the red-haired cannibals were abroad.

The mesa was miles from where the war party had camped the night before. But the cannibals prowled far and wide, as the tracks Nate had come across on the baked plain demonstrated. They were bound to know about the mesa, bound to visit the valley regularly.

Every predator lived by a basic rule: Go where the prey is. And for the cannibals, their prime prey was human beings.

Nate checked on the warriors. They were roving up the mountain hundreds of yards away and posed no threat.

Propping his chin on his hand, Nate gazed at the tribe's sanctuary. Winona and Evelyn were up on that mesa somewhere, and before the night was done he would find them. A bold vow, but he wouldn't rest until they were snug in his warm embrace. He remembered all the time he had hugged Winona and swore he could feel the soft contours of her warm body and smell the fragrant scent of her hair.

Adrift in memories, Nate was startled by a loud outcry. One of the warriors was yelling up a storm and waving a whitish object over his head. Others rushed to see what the racket was about.

Whatever the man had found caused an uproar when he showed it to the rest. An angry hubbub ensued as the whole group moved to the road.

Nate couldn't get a decent look at the object until they stopped. The man had a bone, a leg bone, that of either a woman or a child, to go by its size. Gnaw marks were as obvious as the nose on Nate's face. So were strands of flesh; the victim had died recently.

Not long after, the original search party straggled out of the forest and joined their incensed fellows.

The shadows were lengthening, the sun near the western horizon. Several of the men pointed at it, and after a short discussion, every last one tramped off toward their retreat, eager to reach it before dark.

They weren't the only ones. Over the next half an hour, more hunters, women, and children scurried around the bend. Their numbers, and their urgency, grew as the sun sank lower and lower.

The last to go by were two women and a man, each toting several dead rabbits. Snare kills, Nate guessed, since no blood was on the fur.

Nate would love to get his hands on one. A meal was just what he needed to see him through the long night ahead. Ten hours of sleep would help, too, but he might as well wish for a rifle and two pistols and a powder horn while he was at it.

Smoke from a score of cook fires spiraled skyward from the mesa. The tribe was settling in. Soon Nate would have the valley to himself. More or less.

Yawning, Nate closed his eyes. Another half an hour and it would be dark enough. He wondered how Winona was holding up under the strain. Knowing her, extremely well. She had an inner strength he admired, a toughness that always served her in good stead. In every crisis, in every life-threatening situation they had faced, she never panicked, never went into hysterics as many would have done. She was always so calm, so collected, so self-possessed.

So mature.

A lot of women Nate had known were flighty things. Either they were unduly vain and spent hours every day in front of a mirror fussing over how they looked, or they were obsessed with material goods, with the clothes they wore and the carriage they drove and the house they lived in. Oh, they were pretty, and intelligent, even sophisticated, but they had no depth of character. They were as shallow as a dry wash.

Immaturity was to blame. They never learned there was more to life than appearances. They lived for each new fashion craze, each new formal ball or new theater performance. They shunned toil. They avoided hardship.

And therein was the problem. Character was molded by experience. Ironically, hardship was the forge wherein a person's soul was tempered to perfection. So by avoiding hardship, by devoting themselves to a life of ease and frivolity, many women—and many men—never truly matured.

Winona had endured more than her share of adversity. When she was little, she had seen an uncle and aunt slain by Piegans during a raid. Later in life she lost her parents to the Blackfeet. The Utes, the Apaches, the Sioux, had all tried to kill her or take her captive. She had braved drought and flood, tempests and cataclysm.

And she had come out of it all a stronger, more mature person.

Nate was proud of her. So very proud. And so in love, at times like this it tore him apart to think of what she must be going through.

Blinking in confusion, Nate snapped his head up and looked around. The stars were in full bloom, along with a quarter-moon high in the sky. Much too high. He glanced at the Big Dipper and the North Star and realized it was past midnight. He had fallen asleep and slept for hours!

Furious at his lapse, Nate stood and moved toward the dirt road. Precious time had been lost. By now he should have been at the mesa and found a way to the top. Maybe five hours of darkness was left, and it might not be enough.

Damn. Damn. Damn. Nate wanted to beat his head against a tree. He deserved it for being so stupid, so careless. Every delay was costly. He had let Winona and Evelyn down, and he felt an acute sense of shame.

Moonlight bathed the valley. A stiff wind swayed the tall grass as Nate jogged down the middle of the road. It was safer to approach the mesa through the grass, but he had to make up for lost time. The patter of his moccasins was the only sound.

Nate had gone a quarter of a mile when a loud grunt to the north brought him to an instant stop. Crouching, he glided into the grass and slid the tomahawk from under his belt. At the limit of his vision something moved, something squat and bulky.

The cannibal was heading away from the mesa, not toward it, which suited Nate just fine. When it was out of sight he hurried on, but now he stuck to the edge of the grass so he could quickly hide if he had to.

As Nate neared the mesa he slowed to a cautious walk. He scanned the rim again and again but saw no sign of sentries. But there had to be some. Surely the tribe wouldn't be so negligent.

Boulders of varying sizes were strewn about, and Nate crept in among them. He was scouring the cliff for a trail to the top and didn't spy the dark, gaping hole at the base until he was only thirty feet from it. He also spotted a pair of cannibals.

Darting behind a boulder, Nate peeked out. The brutes were facing the opening and hadn't seen him. They were pacing back and forth, and every so often one or the other would stop and utter a loud grunt. What they were up to eluded him until a third cannibal lumbered from the tunnel. In low, guttural tones they talked a while, then, with no forewarning whatsoever, they wheeled and trotted toward the boulders.

Nate jerked back, drawing the bowie. Their ponderous tread grew louder. For a few harrowing seconds he thought they had spotted him, but they ran past without a sidelong glance, heading off up the road.

After waiting a few minutes Nate slunk around the boulder. The tunnel had been left unguarded and was unlit, another monumental oversight. And one he could take advantage of. Looking both ways, he dashed into the opening and pressed against the left-hand wall to listen.

A constant moan reached his ears. But it wasn't voiced by human or bestial lips. It was the wind.

On either side of the entrance were piles of wood and grass. It didn't take a genius to guess what they were for, but Nate left them alone. Lighting a torch would give him away. He'd have the tribe *and* the cannibals down on his head.

The tunnel was inky black, an ominous stygian maw no sane man would enter alone except in broad daylight. But Nate had to. Mental images of Winona and Evelyn pulled him in. He placed each foot down with extreme care, convinced there had to be traps of some kind. Pits, maybe, laced with dozens of spikes. Or deadfalls. How else did the tribe keep the cannibals at bay?

Suddenly Nate heard a scuffling sound and halted. Another cannibal, he thought, but the sound was followed by a tiny squeak. It was a mouse or some other small creature. Smiling, he continued upward.

Nate's imagination played tricks on him. He saw flitting figures where there were none, saw squat shapes that did not exist. An eternity of nerve-jangling suspense ended when at long last the tunnel brought him near the surface. He felt a breeze fan his cheek and knew he was close, although he saw no stars, no hint of sky.

Sliding the bowie into its sheath, Nate held one arm in front of him and advanced to find out why. His fingers brushed a barrier. Logs had been placed over the opening and tightly wedged together. About to push against one to see if it would budge, Nate froze.

Someone had coughed.

Nate quietly groped the logs, seeking a crack, however tiny, and thanks to the breeze, he found one. As he leaned toward it he detected the scent of burning wood and saw a sliver of light. Bending his neck, Nate spied four guards outlined by the dancing flames of a torch. Its glow revealed piles of firewood and grass, just like at the lower opening.

The tribe was craftier than Nate had given them credit for. If the cannibals tried to break through, all the guards had to do was toss a torch or two onto the logs to set them ablaze. Their fear of fire was their great weakness, one the tribe wisely exploited.

Perhaps the cannibals had tried it in the past and been repulsed.

But now Nate was stymied. He had no recourse but to turn around and go back. The mesa was huge, though. There had to be another way to the top, and he would find it. Rotating, he hastened back down.

Nate had gone about halfway when the walls echoed

to bestial grunts and the scuff of callused feet on the stone floor. Cannibals were coming up the tunnel, and he had nowhere to hide, nowhere to go. Without a moment to lose, he did the only thing he could: He flattened at the bottom of the right-hand wall.

The grunts and the scuffling came nearer and nearer. Nate smelled the awful reek of their brutish bodies, his nose tingling as it had the other night.

Suddenly the cannibals were right next to him. Nate saw their hairy feet go shuffling by within an arm's length of where he lay. He didn't move, didn't look up. With a little luck they would keep on going, oblivious to his presence.

But Lady Luck had deserted him. The creatures halted and noisily sniffed the air. A pair of ponderous feet moved slowly toward him.

Glancing up, Nate could tell the cannibal was turning from side to side to better pinpoint his position. It was only a matter of seconds before he was discovered. Battling them was out of the question. The close confines would hamper him, and in no time he would be overwhelmed.

That left flight.

Bolting up off the floor, Nate flew toward the entrance. Snarls and howls erupted, and the cannibals were after him like hounds after a fox. As powerful as they were, they were not exceptionally fleet of foot. They were too heavy, too massive with muscle.

Nate started to pull ahead, gaining five yards, gaining ten. The mouth of the tunnel appeared, a light patch of gray in a black void. Nate ran as if his ankles were endowed with wings, confident he could elude the man-beasts once he was in the open.

That was when a hulking form strode into the opening, another cannibal with an upraised spear.

Nate couldn't stop. The others would be on him within moments. He boldly sprinted straight toward the one blocking the entrance, watching it closely, gauging the distance. The creature saw him and its powerful body hunched forward as it put all its weight into throwing its weapon.

The spear shot toward Nate's chest as if fired from a catapult. Instantly, he angled to the right, shifting as he did so it streaked by within a cat's whisker of his buckskin shirt. Another couple of bounds carried him to the cannibal, and he sought to fly past before it could stop him.

Fingers as thick as spikes streaked toward his arm. Without missing a stride, Nate twisted and slashed the tomahawk in an arc. The keen edge sheared into the creature's thumb and first two fingers, severing them. That would have been enough to dissuade most adversaries, but the cannibal merely grunted and gave chase, blood spurting from the stumps like water from a fire hose.

Nate raced in among the boulders, angling to the south, a glance sufficient to show him the cannibals were falling farther and farther behind. Within ten seconds they were no longer in sight. He ran for another five minutes anyway, traveling along the south base of the mesa in search of another way up, the wind cool on his sweaty face.

A flat boulder offered a convenient spot to rest for a bit. Sinking down, Nate grimaced as painful spasms racked his stomach. The exertion had taken a toll. He needed food, and lots of it, and he needed it soon.

Opening his possibles bag, Nate took out the last piece of pemmican. He wanted to savor it as he had the others, but he didn't have the time to spare. Stuffing the whole piece into his mouth, he allowed himself one minute to catch his breath. That was all. Then, gritting his teeth, he rose and hustled westward.

The mesa's sheer sides, combined with its dizzying height, defied any attempt to scale it—yet another reason the tribe had chosen it as their home. The cannibals couldn't get at them except through the tunnel, which was effectively blocked off at night.

It turned out the mesa was approximately half a mile long. Nate came to a stop and surveyed the west cliff. It was the same as the others, impossibly high, impossibly sheer. Disappointment, and a deep sense of guilt, seared him. He had failed. He had let his wife and daughter down again. He was about to turn and go back to the tunnel when the quarter-moon crested the mesa's rim and splashed pale light over the cliff.

What Nate saw inspired new hope. To verify he wasn't seeing things, that it wasn't an illusion spawned by shadow, he investigated.

At some point in antiquity a second route to the summit had been created, a rock shelf that crisscrossed up the sheer face, carved by those responsible for the tunnel and whatever lay up above. It wasn't much wider than the ledge Nate had been trapped on the night before, and over the intervening years it had been weakened by the pounding of the elements.

Cracks were evident. Parts were missing here and there. For all Nate knew, it might be so unstable it would fracture under his weight. But it was a way to the top, and he couldn't afford to be choosy.

Sticking the tomahawk under his belt, Nate gingerly started up, his right shoulder brushing the cliff. The shelf held, and he climbed to the first bend without mishap. The next section, though, was webbed by twice as many cracks, and about four yards farther on a two-foot section was completely gone.

Nate looked down. He was about thirty feet above the ground. When he reached the next bend he would be sixty feet up. The one after that, ninety. And so it would go, clear to the crest. A fall would splinter bones and rupture organs; the higher he was, the worse it would be. Adjusting the possibles bag so it was under his left arm and wouldn't snag, he sidled upward.

The shelf bordering the gap looked ready to crumble at the slight pressure. Nate inched as near as he dared, then extended his right leg as far as it would go and pushed off with his left. He held his breath as he alighted, expecting the walkway to disintegrate under him, but it held.

At the next bend Nate looked down at the ground again. He shouldn't have. Queasiness assailed him, and he tore his gaze away before he became dizzy. From then on he would only look up. It was safer that way.

The next stretch was intact, and Nate reached the third bend with renewed hope. Only another two hundred and ten feet to go. *Only*. Nate laughed out loud at his optimism. He mustn't become overconfident. Every step was fraught with potential peril.

Venturing higher, Nate saw the most cracks yet. He took another step but didn't apply all his weight. When the shelf didn't buckle, he slid along it as lightly as if he were sliding on thin ice. He was only a couple of feet from the next bend when the last sound he wanted to hear at that juncture wafted from below.

It was a grunt.

At the bottom of the mesa, staring malevolently upward, stood a red-haired cannibal. A wicked grin spread across its devilish features as it dashed up after him. Displaying no regard for its own welfare, it moved three times as rapidly as he had.

Nate pushed on past the bend. He had to reach the top before the creature reached him. His tomahawk and bowie were no match for the brute's spear, not when he couldn't dodge and weave to avoid it.

Huffing like a steam engine, the cannibal pumped its stocky legs faster. Part of the ramp fell away from under it, but all the cannibal did was give a little hop and keep climbing.

Nate's only hope was to be just as reckless and match

the speed at which it was ascending. It meant throwing caution to the wind, which could kill him as readily as the cannibal.

Then Providence lent a hand. Beyond the next bend lay dozens of jagged rocks, large and small, and Nate snatched one of the largest. Leaning out over the edge, he called out, "Hey!"

The cannibal stopped and looked up.

Cocking his arm, Nate threw the rock with all his might. He was trying to hit the creature flush in the face and cause it to fall, but the rock struck it on the temple instead.

The thing never flinched. The rock had all the effect of a spit ball. Its beetling brow knit, the man-brute touched a thick finger to the bleeding gash. It stared for a few moments at the blood dripping down its finger, and a growl rumbled from its chest. Waving its spear in wanton bloodlust, it let out with a roar that would do justice to a grizzly and barreled up after him.

Nate scampered to the next bend and stiffened in dismay. He hadn't thought to wonder where all those jagged bits of rock came from. Now he knew. Five or six feet of shelf were missing. He couldn't go on and he couldn't go back. He was at the cannibal's mercy.

Chapter Seven

Winona King absorbed the shocking revelation calmly, which greatly surprised Ezriah Hampton.

"Didn't you hear me, lady? I just told you the Great Ones plan to feed you to those filthy cannibals." His good eye stopped jerking and bored into her.

"I heard you."

"And you just sit there? Aren't you going to rant and cry like all the rest?" Ezriah surprised her by switching from English to fairly fluent Shoshone. "Maybe you do not understand the white tongue as well as I thought you did."

"I savvy it just fine," Winona said in English. "Tell me more. How is it done?"

The old man's eye lit with amusement and jerked from side to side again. "It's simple. They'll drag you and the little miss, there, down to the end of the tunnel, and truss both of you up like lambs for the slaughter. Right before sunset, this is. Then they'll leave you there for the Dabi-muzza, the Death Devils, to find. As a sacrifice. Sometimes the cannibals take the people, sometimes the bastards eat them right there on the spot." Ezriah chuckled. "Lordy, you should hear them scream! One fella went on for over an hour."

"You find that humorous?"

"I find life humorous. It's one big joke. We're born, we die. What can be funnier than that?"

Winona wasn't quite sure what to make of him. One second he was perfectly lucid, the next he hovered on the verge of madness. "Why is it the Sa-gah-lee have never fed you to the Dabi-muzza?"

Hampton showed his yellow teeth. "They tried, about two months after they brought me here. There was another captive at the time, a Crow, so they drew lots like they usually do and my luck was true to form. They dragged me, kicking and screaming, down the tunnel, and hog-tied me." His tone took on a tinge of terror. "I laid there about an hour, as I recollect, when I heard them coming. Heard those god-awful grunts that put a shiver down your spine. Then they were right beside me, pawing at me, grinning with those pointed teeth of theirs."

"It must have been terrible," Winona said when he stopped.

Ezriah shuddered. "Terrible enough. I thought I was a goner for certain. But then they rolled me onto my back and saw my eye."

"Your eye?"

He touched the thick scar tissue where his left eye had been. "I lost this when the Sa-gah-lee jumped me. I was trapping beaver at the time, raising pelts north of the Green, and they snuck up on me while I was standing in water up to my waist. I fought like hell, but there were too many. In the scuffle, a lance caught me smack in the eyeball."

"I am sorry."

"Don't be. Hell, it ended up saving me. Those mangy

cannibals wouldn't lay a tooth on me. Surprised the be-jabbers out of the Sa-gah-lee, I can tell you that." Ezriah tittered.

"For twenty years they have kept you here? Why don't they let you go?"

"They're afraid I'll lead other whites back to wipe them out." Ezriah darkened with resentment. "And I would, too. If anyone ever deserved to be turned into maggot food, it's these cowardly vermin."

"I can see why you might not think highly of them," Winona remarked.

"Highly?" Ezriah straightened. "Have you any notion of how many poor souls they've fed to the Death Devils over the years? Hundreds, maybe thousands. And why? Because they're too yellow to fight. They'd rather hide up here and give the cannibals a sacrifice now and then so the Dabi-muzza will let them alone for a spell."

"That is why they do it?"

Ezriah was silent several seconds. "The two tribes have an agreement, of sorts. An old warrior, Red Hawk, told me that long ago, back at the beginning of time, the Sa-gah-lee and the Dabi-muzza waged war. They fought for years, and neither side could win. So a truce was set up. A parley was held, and the leaders of the two tribes made a pact. For every sacrifice the Sa-gah-lee give the Dabi-muzza, the Dabi-muzza won't hunt the Sa-gah-lee for a while. Usually about a month or so."

Evelyn's arm crept around Winona's neck. "What are we going to do, Ma? I don't want to be fed to a bunch of cannibals."

"That's what they all say, dearie," Ezriah said, and cackled. "But your time will come."

"Quit scaring her," Winona said.

"What will you do if I don't?" the old man challenged.

"Poke out your other eye."

David Thompson

Ezriah started to laugh but caught himself. "You know, something tells me you would, too. You must be a regular she-cat when you're riled."

"I do what I must to protect my family," Winona stated matter-of-factly.

"If you're going to protect her from the Death Devils, you'd better come up with a brainstorm pretty quick," the old man said sarcastically. "In about a week it will be a full moon. The Great Ones will draw lots to choose between you and the Flathead gals."

"Plenty of time for us to escape," Winona said.

"Think so, do you? I've tried a couple of hundred times and I'm still here. The Sa-gah-lee always catch me and bring me back." Ezriah sighed. "About five years ago I stopped trying altogether. I reckon I'll live out the rest of my days in this wretched place."

"That need not be. The five of us working together can succeed where you have failed."

"Five?" Ezriah's eye swiveled to Evelyn. "Oh. You're including the sprout. She's just a kid. What good would she be?"

"My daughter is quite resourceful. Do not dismiss her out of hand because of her age or size."

"It doesn't matter how clever she is, or how clever you are. We're boxed in up here. There's no way off the mesa except through the tunnel, and it's always guarded. At night they slide heavy logs across it, logs that take two or three men to move. Even if you managed to reach it, you couldn't budge them on your own."

"The five of us could," Winona said.

Ezriah frowned. "Count me out."

"Why? You do not want to escape after all this time?"

"Of course I do!" Ezriah snapped. "I just can't take another disappointment, is all. I've tried and failed so many times, I couldn't bear to fail again."

"Trust me. We will succeed."

94

Ezriah unexpectedly hopped to his feet and grinned impishly. "Ain't you a peach? I admire a woman with confidence, just so it doesn't get me killed. And as miserable as the past twenty years have been, at least I've spent them alive." He ambled on out, muttering to himself and shaking his head.

The Flatheads had huddled on the other side of the room, but now that he was gone, they bustled over and sat.

"You should not go near the crazy one," Spotted Doe said. "He is dangerous."

"We do not trust him," added Eagle Shadow. The younger sister had thinner eyebrows and a slimmer nose than her sibling. "He has threatened to harm us on occasion."

"Why?"

"He accused us of pestering him," Spotted Doe said.

Eagle Shadow nodded. "All we did was ask him questions. He speaks our tongue. Not as well as he speaks yours, but enough for us to understand him." She glanced at the entrance and lowered her voice. "He is a mean, bitter man."

"Can you blame him?" Winona looked around. To her left was a doorway leading into another room. "I have questions of my own." She rattled them off: "Do we all share this dwelling? How often do the Great Ones feed us? Do they post guards at night, or are we on our own?"

"Why should they bother with guards when they block off the tunnel so there is no way down?" Spotted Doe rejoined.

"They feed us twice a day, at morning and sunset," Eagle Shadow said. "And yes, we share this lodge with the crazy one. He sleeps in there." She nodded at the other doorway. "He snores like a bear."

Winona could think of a lot of other questions she wanted to ask, but her eyes were growing leaden. She had gone without a decent night's sleep for so long, her vitality was at a low ebb.

So was Evelyn's. Stifling a yawn, she placed her cheek on Winona's shoulder and said in Flathead, "I'm tired, Mother. I could sure use a nap."

"That is not allowed, young one," Eagle Shadow said.

Spotted Doe embellished. "The Sa-gah-lee do not let us sleep during the day. They think the only reason we would is to try and escape at night. If they catch you, they will punish you by making you go without a meal or two."

One thing Winona needed was food. She had to get her strength up; either tomorrow night or the next she would make her bid for freedom. "Are we permitted to go where we please during the day?" Keeping busy was the best way to stave off sleep until sunset.

"Yes. Would you like us to show the two of you around?" Eagle Shadow eagerly asked.

"Very much," Winona said.

Their first stop was the central square where dozens of Great Ones had laid out mats and placed various items on them: dead rabbits and squirrels, chunks of deer meat, roots, acorns, herbs, edible plants, and much more. Other Great Ones strolled about examining what was on display.

"They do this every day at the same time," Spotted Doe revealed. "Those who have extra food barter it for things they want."

"But they will not let us take part," Eagle Shadow said. "It is only for members of the tribe."

Winona gazed at the adobe tower. "What is in there?"

Spotted Doe turned. "A ladder to the top, and little else. The Sa-gah-lee do not go in it. They say it is not safe."

Eagle Shadow impulsively clasped Winona's hand. "Come. There is a lot more for you to see, and there is not much time. We must head to our lodge as soon as the sun starts to go down."

"Dawn to dusk, that is the rule," Spotted Doe said resentfully.

The city was divided into districts. In the center were residential dwellings, uniform in construction, single-story or two stories in height. To the north were the tall structures Winona had spied from outside the east gate, the tallest half as high as the tower but all of them imposing in their own right. On the south side of the city was a mix of buildings, no two exactly alike, most in much better shape than those elsewhere. Winona had the impression they had been built last, shortly before disaster befell the occupants.

"Most of the Great Ones live in this area," Spotted Doe disclosed. "The married ones, that is. Women and men who have not married are required to live apart from the rest." She jabbed a thumb at a tall edifice not far from the tower. "The women live in that lodge, the men in the lodge behind it."

"Unmarried women are not permitted to live with their parents?" Winona said. The edict was unthinkable to Shoshones, who placed a premium on family. Unmarried women always lived with their mothers and fathers.

"No," Eagle Shadow said. "Not if they have seen sixteen winters. The Sa-gah-lee say that the Dabi-muzza like to abduct women more than men, especially young women. It has something to do with female flesh being tastier."

"So the Sa-gah-lee put all their eggs in one basket," Winona said. "The easier to protect them, no doubt."

"Eggs?" Eagle Shadow said.

"A white expression. Show me more."

The high wall completely surrounded the city. At regular intervals it was inset with doors, which were kept barred every hour of the day and night. Near each door a flight of stairs led to a parapet much like those at frontier Army forts.

"Come see the view," Eagle Shadow said, and scooted up.

A breathtaking panorama spread before Winona's marveling gaze. From that altitude the valley floor seemed to be on the bottom of the world. The majestic mountains that secluded the valley from the outside world were aglow with the golden rays of the sinking sun, and doubly imposing.

"I feel as if I could flap my arms and fly," Eagle Shadow said. "I love to stand up here for hours, just looking."

"I don't," her sister said crisply. "It reminds me of how far we are from home, and of our loved ones who have cried themselves to sleep in misery over our disappearance."

"You will see them again," Winona declared.

"So you keep saying," Spotted Doe said. "But you must excuse us if we are skeptical. You are one woman and the Sa-gah-lee are many." She folded her arms across her chest. "The Dabi-muzza are many, too, and they worry me more. Even if we escape from the Great Ones, the Death Devils will be waiting for us."

Winona sought to lighten her mood by saying, "They are men, are they not? And I have yet to meet the man women cannot outwit. My grandmother used to say the Great Mystery balanced things out by giving men great strength and women great minds."

The sisters laughed. Evelyn was too tired to do much more than smile.

Eagle Shadow placed a hand on Winona's shoulder. "You are a remarkable person, Winona King of the Shoshones. For the first time since the Great Ones abducted us, I have hope we will truly see our loved ones again."

"I, too," Spotted Doe begrudgingly admitted.

The sun had brushed the peaks. Soon it would van-ish. "We better go back," Eagle Shadow said. "If we are not there when they bring our meal, we will go hungry."

"Then let us hurry," Winona said. "My daughter and I cannot go another night without food."

They barely made it. They had just entered when a pair of Sa-gah-lee women showed up bearing a large clay pot and five clay bowls. Without comment the women set the vessels down and left.

Winona bent over the pot. It was filled with a curious mixture, a soup consisting of bits of meat, pieces of root, and lumps of dough in a thick brown sauce, or gravy. "What is this called?"

"Pig slop." From out of the other room walked Ezriah Hampton. "When you've had it day in and day out, month after month, year after year, you grow to hate it with a passion."

"They must vary the meals from time to time."

Ezriah's eye rolled toward the ceiling. "Listen to her. Hasn't been here a day and already she's knows better than me." Shouldering Winona aside, he helped himself to a bowl and tilted the pot to fill it. "This is their main fare. What most of them eat most of the time. And what they always feed their prisoners." He raised the bowl to his lips and sipped. "Mercy, what I wouldn't give for a nice juicy steak! Or an apple pie! Sometimes when I dream at night, I dream about food."

"When we reach my cabin I will cook you venison steak and bake you a berry pie," Winona offered. "How would that be?"

In the act of taking another sip, Ezriah turned to stone. "You would do that for me? Straight tongue?"

"Of course. I always do what I can to make our guests feel at home, as my husband would say."

"Venison steak and berry pie," Ezriah said softly in undisguised awe. "I'd do anything for a meal like that. Anything you wanted."

"All I ask is that you help us escape," Winona said. His aid would be invaluable. He had been in the lost city for so long, he must know every street, every building, every hidden nook and cranny.

Ezriah's wrinkled features hardened. "I should have known there would be a catch. Dangle a carrot in front of me as if I'm a mule and think I'm too stupid to catch on."

"We cannot do it without you," Winona said. Maybe they could, but his involvement boosted their chances. "And if we never escape, you never enjoy the steak and pie. It is that simple."

"See these white hairs of mine?" Ezriah said, plucking at his beard. "I didn't fall out of the sky with the last cloudburst. Nothing in life is simple, lady. About the time we start taking it for granted, that's about the time life jumps up and bites us in the behind."

"So will you help?"

The old man chortled. "You're a caution. Devious, too. But womenfolk have always been shifty critters, ever since Eve in the Garden of Eden."

Winona knew the story well. Nate owned a Bible and read aloud from it every night. "What did Eve do that was so devious?"

"She ate of the forbidden fruit, didn't she?"

"I thought she was tricked into it."

Ezriah Hampton snorted. "When was a woman ever tricked into anything? No, Eve wanted to eat that fruit. She had it all planned out." Holding his bowl so it wouldn't spill, he sat cross-legged.

"What was her plan?"

"Don't you remember? How Adam and her were traipsing around the Garden in the altogether? How they didn't wear any clothes? No britches or nothing?"

"My husband says they were living in a state of innocence."

"Sure they were. And Eve didn't like it one bit. No,

100

sirree. So when that serpent Satan slithered up and offered her a way to change things, she leaped at the chance."

"I have lost your trail," Winona confessed.

Hampton took a sip, smacked his lips, and continued. "Before I headed west to trap, I had a gal. A pretty filly she was, as sweet as the year is long. Naturally, being a woman, she also liked to nag me to tears and was forever pointing out my faults. And like every other woman, she loved to shop for clothes and such. She'd spend hours nosing into every shop there was and fingering the merchandise."

Winona still did not see the connection. "What does all that have to do with what Eve did in the Garden?"

"I'm getting to that," Ezriah said. "That's another flaw women have. They're too danged impatient."

"Men have no room to talk."

His eye narrowed. "Are you saying men have faults, too?"

"Are you claiming they do not?" Winona countered. "Men are much too stubborn, for one thing. They are much too prone to anger. And they always think they know what is best even when they do not."

"Says you. Remember, the Almighty created men first. That makes men better than women."

"Or it could be the Almighty saved the best for last."

Belly laughs burst from Ezriah, and he rocked back and forth in an excess of merriment. "Oh, that was a gem, ma'am! You're downright comical. If there was a job for telling jokes, you'd be a natural at it."

"Thank you. Now, you were saying about Eve?" Winona prodded. Despite herself, she was curious.

"Oh. Well, she was no different from you or my gal or any other female critter. She had the same hankerings, the same failings. So you can imagine how bored she must have been."

"In the Garden of Eden? I thought it was the most perfect place that ever existed!"

"Hardly. What did Eve have to do all day? She walked around admiring the plants and the animals. That was all there was. Hellfire, after a hundred years or so she must have been bored out of her mind."

"Go on."

"There weren't any of the things women really like to do. There weren't any stores, any shops, any dressmakers. There weren't even any other women for her to gossip with. So when that serpent gave her a notion, she lit on it like a Comanche on a mustang and went right off and grabbed her a heap of forbidden fruit to munch on."

"You're saying she did it on purpose? To what end?"

"Why, to get God mad at her, of course."

Winona stifled a laugh in order not to offend him. "You must have read a different Bible than the one my husband owns."

"They're all the same. Read the story for yourself. Read between the lines, like I did, and you'll see I'm right."

"But why would Eve want to make God mad?"

"So she could go shopping."

This time Winona was unable to contain herself. She laughed heartily, and so did Evelyn. Thankfully, Ezriah simply smirked until they were done.

"Poke fun all you want, but there's no denying the truth. Don't you remember what happened? When the Almighty found out, he booted Adam and Eve out of the Garden. They were free to roam the land, to do whatever their little hearts desired. And what's the first thing they did? They went looking for clothes to wear."

"I do not remember that part."

"It says it right in the Bible. How they covered themselves because they were all ashamed. They were the first shoppers. And womenfolk have loved shopping ever since."

Winona began to wonder if Ezriah truly were addle-pated. "If this is true, why is it men do not like to shop as much as women do?"

"Because men never wanted to be kicked out of the Garden. We still think like we did back then. All we want is to be out among the animals and trees. That's why men like to hunt and fish more than anything else."

Winona grinned. A thread of sanity was woven into his absurd assertions. It was true men were not fond of shopping. Or, to be more specific, they liked to shop only if it took under five minutes. Any longer than that, and they fidgeted and groused and made snide comparisons between women and turtles. Her Nate was no different. On their visits to Kansas City and St. Louis she had wanted to explore every store. He tagged along, insisting it was the right thing for a husband to do. But he couldn't stop grumbling about how long she took.

"If there's any other Scripture you're unclear on, you just let me know," Ezriah commented. "I'll set you straight."

"The one thing I still need to know is whether you will help us," Winona said.

"You're asking a lot, lady. It could get me killed."

"It could also earn your freedom, and that steak and pie you crave."

Hampton stuck a finger into his soup, licked it, and said, "My supper is getting cold. I should be eating instead of jabbering."

"You are stalling."

"And you're pushing me," Ezriah responded irritably. Sighing, he gazed out the front doorway at the gathering twilight. "You know, after all these years, I've sort of gotten used to living as I do. I gave up trying to get away long ago. But now you come along with your pretty smile and your devious ways, and all of a sudden you've got me thinking we just might pull it off."

"We will," Winona declared.

"See what I mean? If wishful thinking was gold, you'd be richer than old King Midas. But I must be as touched in the noggin as you are. Because, damn my soul, you can count me in. We'll bust out of here or die trying!"

Chapter Eight

Nate King had to act. At the rate the cannibal was barreling upward, it would reach him within seconds. Since the creature's spear was a lot longer than his Bowie and tomahawk, the outcome was foreordained. All the brute had to do was stay out of reach and keep thrusting until Nate was impaled or forced over the edge.

The only alternative was for Nate to keep climbing, and he would have except for the five-foot hole in the ledge. Ordinarily, it wouldn't be much of a jump. But the shelf was so unstable that even if he made the leap, he stood the risk of having it break. And it was a long way to the bottom.

A hideous growl from below drew Nate's gaze to the cannibal's contorted countenance, and was just the incentive he needed. Backing up a stride, he coiled, then spurted forward like a runner at a footrace. He took three long steps and hurled himself into the air.

For a few dizzying moments Nate was suspended

David Thompson

more than a hundred feet above the earth. With a sharp crack his moccasins slammed onto the shelf and he pitched onto his hands and knees. He saw fracture lines spreading like a prairie wildfire. At any instant the shelf could give way.

Scrambling upright, Nate ran to the next bend. As he reached it he glanced back.

The cannibal was at the brink of the five-foot gap. As bestial, as primitive as the unholy abominations were, it nonetheless possessed enough intelligence to realize the peril the jump posed.

Nate wanted it to come after him. The shelf would never bear up under its great weight, and there would be one less monstrosity in the world. Waving his arms, he shouted, "What are you afraid of! Jump, damn you! Jump!"

The creature glared, its lips twitching, its nostrils flared.

"You want me, don't you?" Nate taunted. "Well, here I am! Don't just stand there like the ox you are!"

It wasn't working. The cannibal displayed no inclination to make the leap.

"So you do know the meaning of fear?" Nate said, and laughed at his irrational dread of the brutes. For all their ferocity and prowess, they were prone to the same basic human weaknesses.

Apparently the creature thought his mirth was directed at it. Hissing like a snake, the cannibal bared its fangs and moved back a couple of paces.

"You're really going to do it?" Nate said hopefully.

The man-beast exploded into motion, springing up and outward, the incredible power in its steely sinews carrying it past the hole by a good three feet. It landed well beyond the point where Nate had, well beyond most of the fractures, but that wasn't enough to save it.

The shelf splintered and dissolved as if struck by a sledgehammer.

Yet even as the stone crumbled, the creature vaulted forward. Executing a sensational acrobatic flip, it came down on its hands and feet as lightly as a feather. And this time the shelf remained intact.

Nate had blundered badly. Instead of standing there, he should have hastened higher. Now the cannibal was only six feet away and rising, its spear pointed at his chest. He turned to get out of there, but the thing was on him in the blink of an eye, roaring mightily.

Backpedaling, Nate blocked a low thrust with the tomahawk while unlimbering his bowie. He used the knife to ward off a slash that would have opened his gut inches deep, used the tomahawk again to spare his neck from a vicious jab.

The cannibal did not take kindly to being thwarted. Shrieking in outrage, it unleashed a rain of blows, a lethal downpour no adversary could long resist. It thrust. It slashed. It hacked. It was a two-legged cyclone. Unstoppable. Unassailable. A primordial force personified.

But Nate managed to avert death, the bowie and tomahawk always in motion, always blocking, countering. He dodged a stab to the groin by retreating around the bend, and now he was higher than his foe. Instead of giving him an edge, though, it put him at a disadvantage: The lower half of his legs was vulnerable.

Nate jumped straight up as the spear flashed at his feet. It missed, but as he came back down his left ankle grazed the spear and he tripped. His legs were swept out from under him, throwing him onto his back.

The cannibal reared like a colossus of old. It thought it had him dead to rights, and it sneered in triumph as it swept the spear overhead for a fatal stab.

In pure reflex, Nate drove his right foot up into the deer hide at the junction of the creature's stout legs.

A strangled groan tore from the monster's lips, and it doubled over.

Heaving onto a knee, Nate swung his tomahawk at the creature's head. His intent was to split its cranium like rotten fruit, but the tomahawk had shifted in his grip when he fell and it was the flat of the tomahawk that connected, not the razor-sharp edge. Still, the cannibal was jolted backward, nearer the rim, and Nate quickly pounced, determined to finish the brute off before it could recover.

The man-thing, however, had other ideas. Unleashing a roar that blistered Nate's ears, it unfurled and hurtled at him in demonic frenzy. The spear sheared at Nate's throat, and although he brought up the Bowie to deflect the tip, the force behind the blow was so great that the spear battered the bowie aside and the shaft struck his neck a glancing blow.

Intense pain staggered Nate and he tottered to the left, toward open space. He stopped inches from eternity.

The creature gave him no chance to brace for the next onslaught. With a fierce cry it was on him again, slicing the spear at his abdomen.

Nate avoided being skewered like a boar at a cookout by sidestepping, but it left him open to having the blunt end of the spear whipped into his midsection. He was knocked against the cliff, the back of his head smashing hard, and pinpoints of light flared before his eyes.

Iron fingers clamped onto Nate's throat. His vision cleared and he looked into a pair of hellish eyes ablaze with inner fires. He and the cannibal were nose-to-nose, the brute's fetid breath huffing over his face. In the creature's other ham-sized hand was the spear.

Nate thought he was done for, but his left arm had a will of its own. The bowie sheared up into the deer hide, into the same spot his foot had connected with, sinking in to the hilt.

An inhuman screech keened to the stars. The cannibal jerked backward, tearing the knife from Nate's grip. It grabbed the hilt and wrenched, tearing the steel out, so intent on the knife it was unaware it had jerked back past the edge.

The stocky body tilted steeply. Instantly the cannibal flung itself forward to regain its footing, but the effort was too little, too late.

Nate saw the thing glare at him, saw the burning fires that would never be quenched this side of the grave. Then the creature plummeted, the bowie in one hand, the spear in the other. It smashed into the next shelf, bounced like a ball, and crashed onto a lower one with the impact of a cannonball. Half the shelf collapsed as the creature fell free, tumbling end over end, falling, falling, falling until it slammed into the ground with a thud audible as high up as Nate was.

To Nate's utter amazement, the creature started to rise. It was the mechanical impulse of a body drained of will. Blood-drenched, shattered arms flung outward and the deviate spilled into the dust.

Hurting something awful, Nate slowly sank onto the shelf. The bowie could always be replaced, provided he made it home, but now all he had was the tomahawk. Worse, he couldn't go back down if he wanted to. The shelf the beast had smashed into was almost entirely gone. He had to keep climbing and hope against hope the rest were intact. If not, he would be stranded, just as he had been on the other cliff, only this time he wasn't close enough to the top to climb out.

Despair returned, but Nate refused to give in to it. Unsteadily pushing erect, he shuffled upward. The boost of energy he had received from the pemmican was gone. He was totally drained, totally spent. Every muscle ached, every step was an agonizing reminder of the torture his body had endured.

Nate passed the next bend, and the one beyond. His despair faded. He wasn't all that far from the crest. A couple more turns would do it. Then he rounded another and his world came crashing down.

Half the shelf was gone.

Devastated, Nate sagged against the cliff. Not even a cannibal could jump that far. He was stranded, with no food, no water. In his weakened condition he wouldn't last more than two days, if that.

The likelihood of dying didn't upset Nate all that much. He had long since come to terms with the fact that it was inevitable. Each day brought with it the hope of life and the hovering shadow of death. A shadow harder to avoid in the wilderness, where savage beasts and savage men were always out for blood.

No, what upset Nate was the thought of Winona and Evelyn spending the rest of their lives as captives—or worse. He had tried so hard to save them, and it had all been for naught. All his sacrifices, the nights without sleep, the days without nourishment, constantly pushing his body leagues past its limit, had reaped failure.

"Oh, Winona," Nate said softly, and sank onto his buttocks, his back to the cliff. "My sweet, sweet Winona."

An urge to cry came over him, but Nate resisted and stared up at the stars. "Why? In heaven's name, why?"

Winona and Evelyn didn't deserve their cruel fate. In their entire lives they had never committed an evil deed between them. It was a rank injustice, and Nate found his faith in a benevolent Providence wavering. How could God allow such a travesty to occur? he forlornly asked himself.

Nate knew the answer. The sad fact was that bad things happened to good people. Worth or goodness or other personal factors never entered into the picture. It was the capricious nature of existence. A person could be on top of the world one day and beset by grievous woes the next.

Some folks liked to say that hardship befell only those who earned it, that afflicted parties always did something to bring divine wrath down on their heads. But Nate didn't see it that way. Adversity was like lightning; it struck at random, without warning, and could no more be staved off than old age.

Nate had to keep that in mind. He had to remember that Winona and Evelyn hadn't been singled out for punishment. Their abduction was the result of a combination of random events, not the deliberate decision of a spiteful deity.

Glancing at the missing section, Nate wished he had wings. Unbearably sad, he was about to close his eyes when he noticed something he had overlooked.

The shelf had not broken clean off from the cliff. Jagged spurs remained, protrusions varying in width from two to five inches. Enough of them that they formed stepping-stones, as it were, to the other side.

Nate slowly rose. Maybe, just maybe, he could skip from one to the other and make it across. Cautiously inching forward, he scrutinized each outcropping. A few looked sturdy enough, but the rest didn't appear able to support a sparrow, much less a grown man. Still, if he moved quickly enough, if he didn't apply his full weight, and if he could maintain his balance, he might make it.

If, if, if. No other word in the English language more aptly summed up human existence. Life and death, health and sickness, prosperity and poverty, hinged on the outcome of one *if* after another.

Nate shook himself like a bear coming out of hibernation to clear his head of distracting thoughts. His mind must be clear. He must not let his focus waver. There was no margin for mistake. None whatsoever. The slightest misstep would reap calamity.

Girding himself, Nate tensed, took a few deep breaths, and threw himself toward the nearest outcropping. His toes touched down and he immediately hopped to the next, then to the one after that, never stopping, never slowing, always keeping his body close to the cliff but always conscious that if he bumped against it he would be thrown off stride and pitched to his death.

A short spur cracked under him, but Nate had already pushed off.

As if he were tiptoeing across a stream to avoid getting wet, Nate skipped past several more. Suddenly he saw that the outcropping in front of him was split down the middle. But he had already started his leap. All he could do was pray as his toes made contact and he hurtled to the one beyond. The spur gave way, but he didn't fall with it.

Nate landed on the next and jumped. Nine, ten, eleven were behind him now. Only two were left, two of the smallest, two of the thinnest, two of the most fragile. His left foot smacked down, the crackle of stone was like the crack of a whip, and the spur dissolved to dust and bits. He tried to push off, but there was nothing to push against. Throwing himself at the last outcropping, he came down much too hard, much too fast. It broke too, and now his momentum was nearly expended and he still had a couple of feet to go.

Thrusting his right leg forward, Nate pushed sideways against the cliff. It pushed him outward, but it also propelled him forward, and he alighted on the shelf. Off balance, he teetered, his arms windmilling as he resisted gravity's pull.

For anxious moments life and death waged a tug-of-war. Then Nate lurched forward, tripped, and fell onto his stomach. He had done it! His nerves were jangling and his calves were cramped, and he lay there a long while, until he was composed enough to stand.

Marshaling his energy, Nate continued to climb. He dreaded what he would find around the bend and was immeasurably relieved to find the next stretch of shelf intact. The same with the section above.

Tired to the bone, Nate plodded higher, moving mechanically. He needed sleep, needed food, but both were luxuries he must do without until he found his wife and daughter. The wind fanned his face, growing stronger by the second, much stronger than it had been all night, and he looked up, thinking a storm front was moving in. But the explanation had nothing to do with the weather. He had reached the top of the mesa.

Nate's head and shoulders were above the rim. Grinning, he ran up onto solid ground and sank to his knees, overcome with gratitude. "Thank you!" he whispered to the firmament. Overhead, as if in answer, a shooting star flared briefly to life.

Only a few hours of darkness remained, not much time in which to find his loved ones. Hurrying eastward, Nate was astonished to distinguish the silhouettes of a high wall and, beyond it, higher buildings. It was a city, a veritable city in the middle of nowhere, a city where no city had any right being.

A hundred questions leaped to mind: Who built it? When? Why had he never learned of it before? In all the campfire stories and tall tales Nate ever heard, none made mention of a lost city except for the seven legendary Lost Cities of Gold that supposedly existed far to the south.

Alert for sentries, Nate crouched and padded to the wall. There had to be a door or gate somewhere. Roving to the right, he was almost to the corner when his groping hands discovered a break in the blocks, a recessed door made of wood. He ran his hands over every square inch from top to bottom, but there was no latch. It could only be opened from the inside. Putting his shoulder to the wood, Nate pushed. The door barely gave a smidgen, enough to persuade him it was barred.

Nate jogged on around the corner. He came to another door, likewise barricaded. The same with a third. He was beginning to think he would never find a way in. But a little farther on the wall had partially buckled. Not enough for it to collapse. Just enough so the blocks tilted inward at a severe angle.

After making sure the tomahawk was snug under his belt, Nate clawed upward, his fingers gripping niches between each block, his toes wedged into others. He could never have done it if the wall were vertical. As it was, his purchase was tenuous, and twice he slipped and nearly slid back down.

Nate made it halfway up. He made it three-fourths of the way. His fingers and toes were in torment when he came to the last block, which hadn't buckled. To rise past it, he threw an arm overhead, hooked the rim, and pulled himself the rest of the way.

On the other side was a parapet. Anticipating an outcry, Nate drew the tomahawk, but there was none. Off to the east he spied a circle of flickering flame. A torch, perhaps, the only sign the city was inhabited.

Nate cat-footed to a ladder and descended. Gloom shrouded the buildings, concealing details that might give a clue to their origin. He gathered they were old, products of antiquity, of a time many centuries before the advent of the white man. Possibly even before the coming of the red man. The last vestige of a prior age, a monument to a glory that once was, an enigma no man would ever solve. And a potential death trap for him if he were caught.

Nate crept down a narrow street past structures that seemed to be deserted. Most were without doors, their windows uncovered.

Momentarily, from out of the bowels of a pitch-black building on his left, came the unmistakable sound of someone snoring. Warily slinking to the entrance, Nate heard the heavy breathing of other sleepers. He moved to the next dwelling, but no sounds emanated from within. When he paused at the third, he heard someone cough.

The implication was plain.

The tribe was scattered throughout the city. Nate might bump into one of them at any time. With renewed vigilance he turned left at a junction.

Winona and Evelyn could be anywhere. Since Nate couldn't go from door to door asking, how was he to locate them? Common sense dictated that the Indians had posted guards, so if he found a dwelling with warriors posted outside, that was where his wife and daughter would be. Then again, the tribe was a peculiar lot, and they didn't always do what he would do were the situation reversed.

Winding deeper into a maze of empty streets and byways, Nate began to appreciate the full enormity of what he was trying to do. It was akin to searching for a needle in a haystack. A *giant* haystack. Finding them by dawn would take a miracle.

Nate surveyed the city, musing that perhaps it would be smarter to hole up until sunrise. He could climb a tall building and wait for daylight. Sooner or later Winona and Evelyn were bound to appear. One darkling structure was made to order. It was higher than all the rest, and centrally located. He'd have an unobstructed view in all directions.

Nate slunk toward it, stopping at every noise, however faint. In due course he reached a spacious central square or plaza. To reach the tower he had to cross a wide open space, and first he scoured his immediate vicinity.

It was well he did.

From the east end of the plaza came four warriors. They were yawning with fatigue, and stretching. One turned to gaze back the way they had come.

Gazing down the avenue, Nate saw an opening in the wall, a gate, possibly, and the flickering torch. He also spotted four other warriors.

115

The quartet crossing the square had just been relieved and were on their way home.

Nate wasn't worried they would spot him since they were heading to the southwest. Then two of the men slanted in his general direction. Unsure which street they were bound for, and unwilling to risk being seen, he backpedaled to a blackened doorway. He heard nothing to indicate the dwelling was occupied, and ducked inside.

The warriors appeared. They were in no particular hurry. Talking in hushed tones, they strolled by.

Nate peeked out, marking their progress. They were nearing the next intersection when the soft scrape of a foot behind him caused him to whirl. He hiked the tomahawk but didn't use it.

Standing dumbstruck in a doorway to another room was a child, a boy of ten or twelve. He wore a sleepy look typical of someone who had just woken up. His mouth was agape, a finger pointed as if in accusation.

"I will not harm you," Nate whispered in Shoshone. He was going to try some of the tongues he was less conversant in, but the boy didn't accommodate him.

The youngster screamed.

Nate was outside in three bounds. Down the street the warriors heard the cry and turned. It was too dark for them to see him clearly, but his size alone was enough to convince them he was an enemy. Whooping and yipping like rabid coyotes, they raced back toward him.

The boy was still screaming as Nate pivoted and sprinted for the square. Muffled voices from several of the buildings warned him that others had been awakened. He had to find a place to hide, and he had to do it fast.

Nate reached the square and glanced to the left and the right. The other two warriors were at the southwest corner. They, too, had heard the boy. They, too, caught

116

sight of him and rushed to head him off, adding their yells to the racket.

Wheeling to the north, Nate sped a score of yards—only to dig in his heels when two more warriors materialized out of nowhere. Where they came from, he couldn't say. But now escape was cut off on three sides.

Nate ran toward the street that led to the gate, only to have his flight cut off again. The four men out by the torch had heard the ruckus and several were hurrying into the city.

Above Nate loomed the tower. Thinking to evade his pursuers, he ran around it to an open doorway and slipped inside, hoping no one had seen him. He cast about for a spot to hide, but the room was as bare as a pauper's cupboard except for a ladder that extended up through a square opening in the ceiling.

To hesitate spelled doom. Nate grabbed one of the lower rungs and swiftly climbed. The whole ladder creaked as he shot up through the opening into the next chamber, which was as spartan as the first.

Nate stopped. The ladder went up through yet another opening into yet another room, but he reckoned he had climbed high enough to throw the warriors off the scent. Half a minute later a jumble of voices announced they were right outside the tower. *Keep going!* Nate thought, but it wasn't meant to be.

Furtive movement let Nate know they had entered. He started to swing off the ladder before he was spotted, but a face appeared below and a sharp exclamation motivated him into climbing rapidly toward the next level.

Four or five warriors commenced shouting at once. Nate passed through the opening and paused. Once again the room was bare of furnishings, but it no longer mattered. He no longer needed a hiding place. He needed a spot he could defend against superior odds, and the square opening was ready-made. If anyone

David Thompson

stuck their head up through it, he would bash them with the tomahawk. One man, alone, could hold off a horde of hostiles.

Nate shifted to place his right foot on the floor. Without warning the ladder itself shifted, almost spilling him, and from high overhead and from down below came great rending noises.

The ladder dropped like a boulder.

Nate's left shoulder scraped the side of the opening as he fell through, lancing him with exquisite pain. He tried to leap clear, but his left foot became entangled in the rungs. Grabbing a side rail to steady himself, he yanked his foot free and attempted to jump. Wood splintered, and he had a dizzying impression of the ladder breaking into a hundred fragments, of rungs and rails splintering like so much kindling. Then he was falling through space, an opening underneath him. He flipped to the right to avoid it and only partially succeeded.

A jarring blow to Nate's sternum made the world swim. He felt his legs slipping over an edge and clutched at the floor. A new sensation of falling ended with a staggering jolt to his head and chest. He was on his back, a whirlwind threatening to suck his consciousness into an indigo nothingness.

The last thing Nate saw were unfriendly faces above his own.

118

Chapter Nine

Nate King was clawing his way up out of a black hole in the ground. Frantic to reach an oval of light overhead, he tore at the sides in berserk abandon. Muffled voices reached his ears, and faces bobbed above him like apples bobbing in water. He thought they were the same spite-filled faces he had seen before he passed out, and he surged upward in cold fury. He would batter them aside and escape! Nothing would prevent him from saving Winona and Evelyn! *Nothing!*

"Husband, be calm. It is us. You are safe."

Blinking in confusion, Nate realized it was daylight. Sunshine streamed through a window to his right. In front of him, holding his forearms, was the loveliest woman in all creation, her eyes mirroring anxiety and devotion. On his left was a bundle of vinegar and vim, grinning from ear to ear. "Winona? Evelyn?" he blurted uncertainly. "Is this a dream?"

"It is real, husband," Winona answered huskily, letting him go. Choked with emotion, she felt her eyes brimming with tears of joy. "You had a nightmare. You were shouting, and then you sat up and tried to stand."

"You've been hurt, Pa," Evelyn said. "You took a fall, and you've got a bump on your noggin the size of a horseshoe. We were worried you might not pull through."

Dumbfounded, Nate put one hand on his wife and another on his daughter and slowly pulled them to him. "God in heaven! You're both alive!" He embraced them, hugging them close, confirming they were really there and not figments of his overwrought imagination. "I've found you! I've found you!" Tears poured down his cheeks, and his broad shoulders heaved in racking sobs.

"Tarnation, mister. I never saw a grown coon blubber like a baby before. It's downright embarrassing for those of us manly types."

Startled, Nate realized they weren't alone. A white-haired oldster was a few feet away watching in amusement, and a pair of Flathead women stood politely to one side, smiling. Stifling his sob, annoyed by the remark, he rasped, "Who the hell are you?"

"Whoa there, big fella?" the old man said, stepping back. "I didn't meant to rile you. Blubber all you want. To each their own, I always say."

Winona had an arm around her husband and her cheek on his shoulder. "Ignore him," she said, lightly kissing Nate's neck. "His name is Ezriah Hampton. He is also a captive of the Sa-gah-lee."

Nate didn't appreciate having their reunion ridiculed. "Find something else to stare at," he said curtly.

Ezriah glanced at Winona. "You didn't tell me you were married to a grump, lady. What's he do? Eat nails instead of food?" Chuckling, he shambled toward a doorway across the room.

The Flathead women took that to mean they were not wanted either, and they hustled out a door to the outside.

"Now you've done it, Pa," Evelyn said. "You've scared off the only friends we have." Giggling, she kissed his cheek. "But I love you all the same."

"I love you, too. Both of you. So, so much." Nate pressed them to his chest, a constriction forming in his throat, his nose congested. For the longest while the three of them simply sat there holding one another and quietly weeping. They might have sat there the rest of the day had it not been for another caustic comment by the man Nate thought he had shooed off.

"This is really touching and all, friend. But you've been sniffling up a storm for over an hour. Isn't it about time we talked about how we're going to get the hell out of this damnable city?"

Nate raised his head. "Didn't your folks ever teach you any manners?"

Ezriah Hampton had his hands on his scrawny hips and the eyebrow above his good eye arched. "Look, mister, I'm happy for you and your kin. I truly am. But it will be dark in half an hour, and your missus said we might try to escape tonight. If that's so, we need to palaver a bit, don't you reckon?"

"Dark?" Nate repeated in shock. "Do you mean I was out all day?"

Hampton snorted. "All day? Try two days. The Great Ones brought you in here yesterday morning along about sunrise. Told us you tried to climb the tower." He cackled. "Talk about dumb stunts. The ladder was nearly rotted clean through, and no one had been up there in ages."

"It was dark. I didn't know," Nate said absently, stunned by how long he had been unconscious.

"We were awful worried, Pa," Evelyn said. "For a while we thought you might die. And with the full moon just a few days away, we need you."

"The full moon?" Nate looked at his wife.

Winona explained, and went on to detail everything

she had learned since being taken captive, all she knew about the Sa-gah-lee and the Dabi-muzza and the lost city of the Old Ones. As she was finishing, Spotted Doe and Eagle Shadow came back in and she made the introductions.

"Our hearts are happy to meet you, Grizzly Killer," Eagle Shadow said. "Your woman has told us much about you, about your courage and wisdom. Surely, with your help, we can escape this terrible place."

"We'll do it or die trying," Nate declared.

"Speak for yourself, friend," Ezriah responded. "Me, I'm partial to breathing. I'll help out, but I'm not going to be turned into wolf bait. Being alive is better than breathing dirt any day of the week."

"He is always this cynical, husband," Winona said. Rising, she bent over Nate's head. "I want to examine you." She gently parted his hair and ran her fingers over the bump and the area around it. The swelling was a lot less, but not enough to suit her. "You must take it easy for a day or so," she suggested.

"With the full moon so close? Not on your life." Nate put both hands on the floor and shoved upward. Suddenly a tidal wave of intense dizziness and nausea flooded through him, rendering him so weak he collapsed onto his back with a loud groan.

"Too soon, husband, much too soon," Winona chided. "You need a lot more rest. Please just lie still."

Nate frowned in frustration. He had finally tracked down his loved ones, only to be in no shape to help them. As if to accent the point, his stomach rumbled like a steam engine with a busted piston.

"When did you last eat a meal?" Winona inquired.

"Seven or eight days ago, I think."

"You think?" Winona was appalled. He had a habit of ignoring his bodily needs when those he cared for were in danger. "Even more reason for you not to exert yourself. The Great Ones will feed us soon. They do not give us a lot, but you can have as much as you want. We will not mind."

"Speak for yourself," Ezriah interjected. "It may not be the tastiest hog slop, but it's all we get. And I, for one, don't intend to go hungry on your husband's account."

Winona controlled her temper with an effort. "The sooner Nate recovers, the sooner we can leave. And the sooner you will get your steak and pie. Or have you forgotten?"

The old man smacked his lips. "Forget about a feast fit for a king? It's all I've been thinking about since you brought it up."

Nate's stomach-ache had subsided, but the vertigo refused to go away. He lifted his right arm to see if his strength was returning and was horrified when he couldn't raise it more than an inch. His body was completely drained of energy. Exhaustion was to blame. Near-total exhaustion.

Ezriah looked at him but addressed Winona. "So how long do you figure it will take this hubby of yours to get back on his feet?"

Nate answered for himself. "By tomorrow night I'll be fit enough."

"That soon?" Ezriah said. "Pardon me for being a Doubting Thomas, but you're as pale as a sheet and as puny as a newborn. Too bad we don't have a mirror handy, hoss. One look and you'd scare yourself silly."

Sighing, Winona glanced up. "Must you?"

"What did I do?" Ezriah rejoined.

Evelyn had not budged from Nate's side. Putting her lips to his ear, she whispered, "I've missed you so much, Pa. I was afraid we'd never see you again." She paused. "What happened to the Shoshones you were with? To Only Hunts Elk and Rabbit Tail and all the others?"

"They're gone."

"Dead? Every last one? How?"

David Thompson

Nate preferred to spare her the gory details. The warriors had met violent gruesome ends that would haunt him for years. "Let's just say that Bear Canyon lived up to its reputation and let it go at that."

"I liked Rabbit Tail," Evelyn said sadly, speaking of the youngest, a youth not much older than she was. "At least tell me how he died."

Winona came to Nate's aid. "Another time, perhaps, little one. When we are home safe, your father will tell you all about it."

"Ahhh, Ma."

A welcome interruption came in the form of two middle-aged Sa-gah-lee women carrying a steaming clay pot and bowls. The women deposited them without comment, retrieved vessels left from that morning, and departed.

"Now we will get some food into you," Winona told Nate. She poured a helping for Evelyn, then filled another bowl and sat back down. Slipping a hand under his head, she carefully elevated him high enough to suit her purpose and touched the bowl to his lips. "Eat slowly," she cautioned.

Nate's mouth watered in keen relish. He took a tentative sip. To say it was delicious did not do it justice. He chewed a few times, relishing the flavor, then swallowed. Almost immediately his stomach did flip-flops, and for a few seconds he thought the morsel would come up again.

"What is wrong?" Winona demanded. His whole body had tensed up, and his throat had bobbed as if he were choking.

"It's been a while," Nate said. He waited until the sensation passed and took another sip. This time he chewed twice as long, and when he swallowed, he was braced for another upheaval. But his body didn't rebel.

"Doing better?"

"I could eat a bull elk," Nate quipped, and cheerfully

polished off the rest of the bowl. Soon renewed energy pulsed through his body. He would have sat up, but he was much too content and comfortable nestled in Winona's lap.

Ezriah Hampton and the Flatheads were also partaking, Hampton by himself near the opposite wall. "So tell me, mister. You must make your living as a trapper. Are plews still fetching top dollar?"

"Not anymore," Nate said. "Fashions have changed. The beaver trade is drying up. Rumor has it that in another year or two it will be pretty much over."

Hampton's jaw dropped. "There's no more market for hides? What happened to all the trappers?"

"Most died," Nate said. Of approximately three hundred who had plied the mountains at the beginning of the trapping boom, fewer than a dozen remained. "Some went off to explore California and liked it so much they stayed. Others went back east. A few, like me, built homesteads."

Ezriah couldn't get over it. "The beaver trade, dying out! I never thought I'd live to see the day. How do you make ends meet, then?"

"Any way I can. I've scouted some for the army. I've guided emigrants over the Oregon trail—"

"What trail?"

"A wagon route from the Mississippi River to the Willamette Valley in Oregon Country. Thousands of pilgrims have gone there to start new lives, and the government expects thousands more will do the same before the turn of the century."

"I've missed a lot while I've been away, haven't I?" Ezriah said. "Who's the president nowadays?"

"Martin Van Buren."

"Never heard of him. Last I recollect, it was that Monroe fella." Ezriah's good eye drooped half shut. "I was one of the first to come west, you know. Back when beaver first became popular. I had some big plans, I did.

I was going to carve out a fur empire and make a fortune."

"Someone else had the same idea. John Jacob Astor is now the richest man in America."

"The damn scoundrel stole my notion!" Ezriah indignantly declared. "When I get back, I have half a mind to look him up and blow out his wick."

"You'll find a lot has changed," Nate said, and would have gone on if Winona hadn't placed a hand over his mouth.

"Enough talk, husband. I want you to get done eating and then rest."

Ezriah snickered. "It's plain to see who wears the britches in your family. Better do as the little lady says or she's liable to spank you." His joke struck him as hilarious. When he was done guffawing, he commented, "Too bad, though. I was hankering to hear what else is new."

Winona had removed her palm to refill Nate's bowl. "This is the last of it." She didn't bother to mention that she had eaten half as much as she usually would so there was more for him.

Nate tested whether he could lift his arm and was delighted to find he could. To Hampton, he said, "How long have you been away?"

"Two decades, give or take a few months. Mississippi had just become the twentieth state, and work was started on some big canal."

"The Erie Canal," Nate said. "Long since completed. Steamboat travel is all the rage nowadays. They even ply the Mississippi and Missouri Rivers."

"You don't say."

"What else might interest you?" Nate tried to remember events of major importance that had occurred since Hampton was taken captive. "Texas is a Republic and wants to be admitted to the Union, but Congress won't let it."

"Why not?"

"There's been a movement afoot to oppose slavery in the South. Northern congressmen are afraid if they admit Texas, it will join the pro-slavery states." Nate pondered a bit. "The United States now has about fifteen million people. New York City is the biggest, with close to two hundred thousand."

"Good God!" Ezriah exclaimed. "They must be piled three deep in the streets."

"Some fellow named Colt has invented a new type of gun called a revolver. I haven't seen one yet, but I hear it fires up to six shots without reloading."

"Impossible."

Nate recalled accounts from newspapers he had obtained in trade with pilgrims bound for Oregon. "You think that's strange? A scientist says there's vegetation on the moon, and where there's vegetation, there might be intelligent life. School for women are springing up, and women are pushing for the right to vote." He thought of another. "A new sport is becoming popular. They call it baseball. I saw a game once in St. Louis. They put four stones twenty yards apart on a square field. Then a man stands in the middle and throws a little ball at another man holding a stick. If the fellow with the stick hits the ball, he runs to all the stones and touches them with his foot."

"The world sounds as crazy as ever," Ezriah said dryly. "It's nice to know some things never change."

Nate wasn't done. "There's a new kind of steel plow that farmers say makes their job ten times easier. A gent named Webster has published a dictionary of the American language. And water closets are being put in all the finest hotels."

"Why would they want to keep water in a closet? What's wrong with getting it out of a well?"

"It's not that kind of water closet. It replaces chamber pots."

Hampton was flabbergasted. "The devil you say! I'll be damned if I'm going to sit in water when I heed Nature's call! Dry land suits me just fine. What maniac came up with such a loco idea?"

Before Nate could elaborate, into their dwelling filed four warriors. In the lead was the man with the headband. Nate also recognized the others as being part of the war party.

Winona grew alarmed. The stern expression Hawk wore did not bode well. Stone was with him, as were Antelope and Broken Stick. They faced Nate, and her heart fluttered in secret fear they intended to do him harm.

Nate had seldom felt so helpless. He wanted to rise, to confront them, but he couldn't do it on his own and he didn't want them to know how weak he was. So he compromised and sat up, the effort straining him.

Hawk glanced at Ezriah Hampton and beckoned. Taking his sweet time, the cantankerous old trapper rose and shuffled over, his eye jerking spasmodically. Hawk spoke to him for a minute.

"He has some questions to ask you, King, and he wants me to do the honors," Ezriah said. "He knows your wife has learned a little of their tongue, but I speak it as well as they do, so I can do a better job."

Winona stirred, thinking of a question she had been meaning to ask. "All these years, and yet you have not taught any of the Sa-gah-lee English?"

Ezriah hooked his thumbs in his breechclout. "Why should I do the Great Ones any favors? I hate the bastards."

Hawk was studying Nate and Winona, and said something.

"He wants to know if the two of you know each other," Ezriah translated. "I guess he figures the lady wouldn't have her arm around just any stranger who happens along." Ezriah paused. "What do you want me to say?"

128

"Does it put my husband in danger if we tell the truth?"

"Not that I can see, no."

"Then go ahead."

The old man obeyed. It sparked a heated discussion between Hawk and Broken Stick. At last Hawk turned to Ezriah.

"How did your husband find you?"

"I'll answer for myself," Nate said. "Tell him I tracked them here from the spring where he took my wife and daughter."

"He says you must be some tracker. How did you reach the top of the mesa?"

"I climbed the west side."

"Up that old trail carved out of rock?"

"From bottom to top."

"Hawk says you're a liar. And frankly, mister, so do I. I've been there. I've seen it. The rock is all cracked, and broken in parts. No one in their right mind would try such a harebrained stunt."

"I'm here, aren't it?"

"Hawk wants to know how you got into the city."

"I climbed the wall."

"You must be part squirrel," Ezriah bantered. He relayed the answer to the tribe's leader and Hawk posed another question. "How did you get past the Dabi-muzza? The cannibals?"

"It wasn't easy. They caught me once, and almost had me a second time. I left two dead and wounded a third."

"You slew two Death Devils? By yourself? Hawk thinks you're lying again. The Dabi-muzza are too strong, too fierce. It takes ten men to kill just one."

"They are strong, yes, but they are human, like us. They bleed. They die."

"Did you kill them with a thunderstick? A gun?"

"All I had was my knife and tomahawk. If I'd had a rifle or pistol, it would have been a lot easier."

"Hawk says it wouldn't make a difference. He saw a white-eye shoot a charging Death Devil once, and the Death Devil still thrust a spear through the white's body."

"The man must have missed a vital organ. He should have shot it in the head." Nate stared at Hawk, suspecting there was more to the queries than simple curiosity. He had seen how fearful the Sa-gah-lee were of the Dabi-muzza. Even here, in their sanctuary, they were deathly afraid the cannibals would somehow reach them. "Ask him if his tribe is tired of living like timid rabbits."

Ezriah balked. "He might not take kindly to having his people called cowards."

"Do it."

Winona wondered what her husband was up to. She saw Hawk's mouth compress into a thin line. Broken Stick flushed with anger and snapped a response.

"What did that one say?" Nate asked.

"He wants Hawk to let him slit your white throat." Ezriah leaned down and lowered his voice as if confiding a secret. "Broken Stick, here, has the sourest disposition this side of a lemon. He hates everyone who isn't a Sa-gah-lee. He and Stone, the one on my right, are both next in line to be chief if Hawk dies. According to tradition, the elders will pick lots. If Broken Stick wins, Lord help any whites they take captive. He'll torture them before he gives them to the Death Devils."

"Has he tortured you?"

"The son of a bitch has wanted to. But Hawk won't let him."

Nate's estimation of the leader rose several notches. "Tell Hawk his people need not be afraid. Tell him they can end the threat of the Dabi-muzza forever."

"He wants to know how."

"By going to war."

Ezriah chortled. "Are you insane? The Sa-gah-lee

wouldn't stand a prayer. Half the men pee themselves just thinking about the cannibals. They'd never stand up to them."

"Just repeat what I said."

Hawk's response was long and detailed.

"He says your words are hollow. A war with the Dabi-muzza would destroy the Sa-gah-lee. They are no match for the cannibals, who only come out at night. The Dabi-muzza can see better in the dark, and they have a much better sense of smell. All his warriors would be slain, and then the cannibals would come for the women and children."

"Why fight the cannibals on the cannibals' terms?"

"How's that, hoss? I don't savvy."

"Tell Hawk I speak with a straight tongue. Tell him the Dabi-muzza have a weakness. They don't like bright light. That's the reason they don't come out during the day. So all the Sa-gah-lee have to do is attack while the sun is up. They'll have the advantage, not their enemies."

"Hawk has had the same idea. But for it to succeed, the Sa-gah-lee must track the cannibals to their lair. And his people are not very skilled at tracking."

"I am," Nate said.

Winona guessed what her man was up to and interrupted. "We can escape on our own, husband. You do not need to do this."

Ezriah was perplexed. "Do what? What's she talking about?"

"Tell Hawk I want to strike a deal," Nate instructed.

"In case you're forgetting, you're his captive. Why should he bother?"

"Because I can help end the reign of terror his people have endured for so long. If he promises to let all of us go, I will track the Dabi-muzza to their lair and help the Sa-gah-lee wipe every last one of them off the face of the earth."

Chapter Ten

The difference a couple of days made was amazing. Plenty of sleep and food had restored Nate King's vitality to such an extent that he felt like a new man. It helped that a great weight had been taken off his shoulders; he was no longer in constant fear of harm befalling Winona and Evelyn.

On the afternoon of the second day after Nate's fall, Hawk was due to pay another in a series of visits. Nate was pacing like a caged painter, aware that the lives of his loved ones were riding on the speech he must shortly make.

Winona was near the window, combing the knots out of Evelyn's hair with a bone comb supplied by a Sagah-lee woman. She disagreed with what her husband had done, but she was not one of those wives who nagged when they did not get their way. She trusted him, trusted his wisdom, and if he thought it best, she would go along with his proposal and do all in her power to help him, not hinder him. "Calm yourself.

They will be here soon. It would not do for you to show you are nervous."

Ezriah Hampton was hunkered in his favorite corner. "Hell, I'd be nervous, too, if I'd stuck my neck on the chopping block. The Sa-gah-lee will never go for it. We'll be no better off than before."

Nate stopped pacing and faced him. "Wrong. If nothing else, I've bought us time."

"Time for what?"

"For me to mend. If they refuse, we'll make our bid for freedom tonight."

"So you had another motive all along?" Ezriah giggled. "Sneaky cuss. I like that." Standing, he wriggled his legs. "I reckon I shouldn't complain. For the first time in twenty years I'm not wearing a hobble."

Nate smiled. None of them were. As a token of goodwill, Hawk had agreed to have the hobbles removed, to give them more food, and provide medicinal herbs to speed his recovery. "Remember to translate my words exactly as I say them. We don't want any mistakes."

"Confidence is the key," Winona interjected. "You must make them believe your plan will succeed."

"It will," Nate said with complete conviction. "If nothing goes wrong."

"But that's the problem, sonny," Ezriah threw in. "The cannibals are as unpredictable as grizzlies. They can be chock-full of nasty surprises. I'd hate to be in your moccasins if they catch you and the Sa-gah-lee outside the city after dark."

"Catch us, you mean."

Ezriah's eye jumped in its socket. "Now hold on there, hoss. I never said I'd tag along on your little escapade. If you want to go off and get yourself eaten, that's your affair. You'll make a dandy main course for the Dabi-muzza. Just don't expect me to be the appetizer."

"Do not let Mr. Hampton hoodwink you, husband,"

Winona said. "The cannibals did not eat him before when they had the chance."

"So? I'm not pushing my luck a second time." Ezriah shook his head. "No, no, no. Not in a million years."

"I can't do it without you," Nate said. "You're the only one who speaks the Sa-gah-lee's tongue."

"Your missus has learned enough to get by. When you waltz off to wage your war, take her along. She can do the translating."

"My wife has to stay here to watch over our daughter."

This was news to Winona. She opened her mouth to object, but thought better of the idea. What else were they to do? Protecting Evelyn was much too important to be entrusted to people they hardly knew.

"Have the Flatheads do it. I'm sure they wouldn't mind," Hampton said. "And to show you I'm not a coldhearted coon, I'll help. What more could you ask?"

Nate said nothing. Arguing was useless. He needed the old trapper's help, and that was that. He regretted what he had to do, but the welfare of his family came before all else.

A commotion outside heralded the arrival of Hawk and half a dozen warriors. The rest waited as the leader strode indoors and formally greeted Nate by placing his right hand on Nate's chest and saying the Sa-gah-lee word for "friend."

Nate reciprocated, then walked over to give Winona and Evelyn a hug and a kiss. "Keep your fingers crossed," he said.

"Our legs, too," Winona responded.

Evelyn wrapped her slender arms around Nate's thick neck and nuzzled her chin against his beard as she had been wont to do since early childhood. "You need a trim, Pa."

Nate's mind flashed back to the last time she had done that. A late-spring chill had spurred him into starting a fire, and he had been seated on the large bear rug in front of their hearth, stoking the flames, when she perched on his knee to ask a question about the Mc-Guffey Reader she was studying. He could still feel the warmth of the hearth, the scrape of her chin, and the abiding sense of peace and security. He would do any-thing—*anything*—to restore the life they had once known.

"Be good for your mother," Nate said, and rose. Hawk had already gone out.

Ezriah was impatiently waiting at the door. "Remember what I said, friend. I'll translate for you tonight. But I'm not going with you if the Sa-gah-lee agree to throw their lives away. And that's final."

The council was being held at the public square, and the entire tribe was in attendance. Over a hundred, by Nate's estimation, the women and children seated at the rear, the warriors in long rows at the front, the oldest men nearest the platform.

Butterflies fluttered in Nate's gut as he climbed the stairs behind Hawk, who stepped to the front and with-out ceremony commenced an impassioned speech.

"Here we go, hoss." Ezriah kept his voice low. "He's thanking them all for coming. He says this day is one that will be remembered for as long as there are stars in the sky—"

"Word for word," Nate said.

"Huh? That's what I'm doing."

"No, you're summing up what he says. Translate it word for word. I need to know *exactly* what they say."

"Do you have any idea how much harder that is?"

"Do it."

"Damn." Ezriah listened a moment, then obeyed. "The Sa-gah-lee take their destiny into their own hands, when we stand up to the devils who have plagued us since the dawn of time. I say it must end! I say we have suffered enough! How many loved ones must we lose?

135

David Thompson

How many wives, daughters, sons, brothers, sisters, friends must be eaten before we rise up against the eaters of our flesh? How long will we go on being scared of the dark? How long will we go on hiding from the truth?" Hawk, and Ezriah, paused. "In a few moments one of our captives will address you through old One-Eye. I beg you to listen to his words. I plead with you to admit them into your heart. And I beseech you to agree to what he will propose."

No one applauded as Hawk stepped back. Nor would they if they were Shoshone, Cheyenne, or Crow. Among most tribes public speeches were always greeted with respectful silence.

Now it was Stone's turn. "You have heard the plea of our leader. I add my own to his. For too long the Dabi-muzza have terrorized us. For more winters than there are leaves on the trees they have preyed on us as wolves prey on deer. They steal those we love, and all we ever find are bones. My people, they must be stopped! We must show the Dabi-muzza we are strong! We must reclaim our honor, our self-respect! We must be worthy of the name Great Ones. So listen to the white man with open ears."

Broken Stick strutted forward. "You have heard our illustrious leader. And you have heard from the one who thinks he is as worthy as I am to take our leader's place one day. What is it they would have of you? Only that you pay heed to the white dog who is about to speak. That does not seem like much to ask." Broken Stick paused for dramatic effect. "Not much at all, until you consider what it is the white-eye is about to propose. I agreed in advance not to reveal what it is, but I can tell you this, my people. If you agree to the white man's plan, you doom the Sa-gah-lee. Our tribe will cease to exist. We will shame the memory of our fathers, and our father's fathers, and all those who have fought to preserve our people since the beginning of time.

136

Choose life, not death! Hear the white dog out, yes, but then laugh in his face for presuming to think he knows better than we how we should live our lives!"

It was Nate's turn. Broken Stick sneered as he stepped to the edge with Ezriah at his side. "Word for word," he reminded the oldster.

"Don't fret, sonny. Just don't be too disappointed when they turn you down. I told you. The Sa-gah-lee are born with yellow streaks down their backs. They're the worst bunch of cowards on the planet."

"You never know about people," Nate said, collecting his thoughts.

"The hell you don't. They've held me captive for twenty years. I know them like I know the back of my hand. The Sa-gah-lee are as worthless as teats on a boar."

Nate scanned the rows of swarthy faces. Most were impassive. A few were blatantly hostile. "I thank Hawk for the honor of allowing me to address you," he began, and paused so Ezriah could convey the statement. "What I have to say is important. Perhaps the most important words you have ever heard. But before I get to that, I must respond to what Broken Stick said." He glanced over his shoulder at the bigot, who placed a hand on a knife at his hip and looked ready to spring.

Not intimidated in the least, Nate continued. "Broken Stick has asked you to choose life, not death. But what sort of life is it when you live in fear? What sort of life is it when you cannot live as you want to live? When you must barricade yourself on this mesa every night? When mothers are afraid to let their children out of their sight? When each year, there are fewer and fewer Sa-gah-lee? Broken Stick claimed that if you listen to me, you doom your tribe. But if you do not listen to me, your people are doomed anyway. Eventually there will not be any Great Ones left."

Nate stopped to let his message sink in. "You all

137

know why. For winters beyond number you have been preyed on by men who are not men. By creatures that delight in eating human flesh. The Dabi-muzza are to blame for all your woes. All your misery. For your fear. For never having enough food to eat. If there were no Dabi-muzza, think of how different your lives would be."

Again Nate stopped. "I am an adopted Shoshone. I have seen how other tribes live. Imagine being able to go about as you please during the day *and* at the night. Imagine children always smiling and carefree. Imagine women able to go for water without having to worry they will not make it back to their lodge. Imagine nights spent seated around campfires telling tales and laughing. Imagine a life that is the opposite of yours, and that is how it could be if there were not Dabi-muzza."

Many a creased brow testified that they were doing just that.

"The Sa-gah-lee have the right to live as they want. To live as other tribes do. But you cannot do that so long as the Dabi-muzza exist. They control your lives. They treat you as if you are a herd of buffalo, to be culled at their whim. They, and they alone, are all that keep you from the happiness that is justly yours.

"The Death Devils will go on terrorizing your people until there are no Sa-gah-lee left. But it does not have to be that way. The Sa-gah-lee need not let themselves be slaughtered off. There is another path you can take. A path that will end the reign of terror. A path that will enable you to live as the Shoshones and others do."

Nate paused, and Ezriah looked at him. "How much longer are you fixing to flap your gums? My throat is getting raw from all this jabbering."

"A while yet," Nate said.

"You'll wear me to a frazzle."

"Hardly. Just keep translating."

"You're wasting your breath."

"It's my breath to waste. And I don't appreciate being interrupted."

"All right. Don't get huffy on me. I'm doing it, ain't I?" Muttering, Ezriah glumly regarded the Indians.

Nate quickly resumed. "There is only one way for the Sa-gah-lee to live as they would like. That is to eliminate the Dabi-muzza. In your hearts you know this is true. So my proposal is simple. You must go to war against the Death Devils. You must live up to your name as the Great Ones and do what your forefathers never could. You must destroy the cannibals so you can once again hold your heads high as a free people."

Their faces never changed expression. No one spoke, no one moved.

"I can guess what some of you are thinking. The Great Ones have fought the Death Devils many times and have never been able to defeat them. Why should now be any different? Why should you risk your lives at the urging of a white man, a stranger?

"Perhaps because I look at the problem with new eyes. I have fought the Dabi-muzza. I have seen two of them die. And if two can die, twenty can die. Forty can die. Sixty can die. You, the Sa-gah-lee, can slay them. With my help.

"I am a tracker. I tracked the warriors who took my wife and daughter from the country beyond the baked plain. What I did then, I can do again. I can track the cannibals to their lair. For the first time in the history of the Sa-gah-lee, you can attack the Dabi-muzza where they live. You can do to them as they have done to you."

Ezriah chuckled. "Great Ones, my ass! Look at them! Like bumps on a log! Everything you say is going in one ear and out the other."

"Don't interrupt again," Nate warned him. To the Great Ones, he said, "Think what it would mean. For once you would have the advantage. For once you have a real chance to put an end to the Dabi-muzza for all time. No more fear. No more lost loved ones. A new age for the Sa-gah-lee will begin."

Nate was just about done. He had said all he could as best he knew how. The next step was up to them. Yesterday, Hawk had told him that in matters of grave importance, it was Sa-gah-lee custom to discuss it thoroughly. Every warrior got to voice his opinion, and either approve or disapprove. As leader, Hawk would abide by whatever the majority decided.

Glancing at Hampton, Nate said, "Ask if they have any questions."

An elderly warrior in the foremost row hiked his hand. "How do we know this is not a trick so you can escape?"

"My wife and daughter will remain here," Nate answered. "After all the trouble I have gone through, do you think I would run off and desert them?"

Another old warrior cleared his throat. "How long will it take to track the Dabi-muzza?"

"I cannot say. It depends on how far away their lair is. But I suspect it is a lot closer than most of you imagine."

"Why do you say that?"

"They come each night, they leave shortly before dawn each morning to return home. So they must not have far to travel."

A third warrior straightened. "No one knows how many Death Devils there are. They might greatly outnumber us."

"If that were true, they would have broken through the log barricade long ago and overrun you. They would steal people from a lot of different tribes, not just Sa-gah-lee. This alone tells me they are not numerous."

"Our weapons are ineffective," a fourth warrior brought up. "Our lances do not always kill them on the first thrust, and our bows fare little better. We have shot arrows into them until they bristle like porcupines, and still they do not fall."

"Of course not. Their bodies are too thick with muscle. That is why we will do it differently."

"How many warriors would you take along?"

"As many as want to come. I suggest leaving ten warriors here with Stone to protect your women and children and have the rest go with me."

"Only ten? What if the Death Devils attack while all of you are away?"

"If we do it right, they will not know we are gone. They will think all of you are still here. By moving fast and striking hard, we can catch them by surprise."

"Why do you do this, white man? Why do you help us when we took your woman and child?"

"Two reasons. Hawk gave me his word that if we succeed, all the captives will be released unharmed."

"And the second reason?"

Nate remembered watching the cannibals devour one of their own. "The Dabi-muzza must be stopped. They are a violation of Nature. Creatures that should have died off long ago. No matter what it takes, we must put and end to these cannibals forever."

Murmuring broke out. Nate stepped back and looked at Hawk. "What now?"

Hampton translated the reply. "You will be taken to your dwelling. My people will debate the merits of your plan, and I will visit you when a decision is made."

Broken Stick moved in front of Nate and barked off a string of sentences, which the old trapper dutifully relayed. "I can tell you now, white dog, they will never agree. The Dabi-muzza would destroy us if we do as you want. You have no business meddling. Our ways are not your ways. As it has been, so shall it always be."

"Doesn't having your own people eaten bother you?"

"Of course. But it is the nature of things. Bears and wolves and panthers kill some of us from time to time, yet we do not rise up and go kill every bear, wolf, and panther we can find. It is how life is."

"I disagree. When we can make our lives better, we owe it to ourselves to try."

"So you say. But it is not the fate of your people that is at stake. It is the fate of mine. And I refuse to let them go off to be slaughtered."

"You show little confidence in the Sa-gah-lee. Maybe they would surprise you. Did you ever think they might win?"

"Leave, white-eye, before I strike you. If I have my way, my people will stake you out tonight for the Dabi-muzza to find instead of waiting for the full moon."

Antelope and Runs Slow were ready to take Nate and Ezriah back. As they wound along the narrow streets, the old-timer nudged Nate.

"I've got to hand it to you, friend. That was some spiel. If it doesn't convince them, nothing will. And if it doesn't, what's our next move?"

"We escape on our own."

"Fine and dandy. But how, exactly? It's not as if we can walk to the edge of the mesa and jump."

"I haven't worked that out yet."

Ezriah's eye widened. "Wait until the last minute, why don't you? I knew I shouldn't have gotten my hopes up. I just knew it." Mumbling under his breath, he sulked the rest of the way.

Winona and Evelyn were waiting out front.

"How did it go, Pa?" Evelyn cried as the pair ran to meet him.

"We'll find out when the council is over." Nate draped his arms across their shoulders. "It could be hours."

"We should go for a stroll while we wait," Winona said. She was tired of being cooped up. And despite all her talk about staying calm, she was too apprehensive over the vote to sit still for very long.

"Count me out," Hampton said testily, going inside.

The two warriors hurried off, eager to take part in the council, leaving Nate alone with two of the four people who were the world to him. "A stroll sounds nice."

With all the Sa-gah-lee at the square, the lost city of the Old Ones was as quiet as a tomb. They meandered deeper into its musty depths, wandering aimlessly, enjoying their idyllic interval together.

"I can't wait to get home, Pa," Evelyn commented as they stood admiring the splash of vivid color in the western sky.

"Can't wait to sleep in your own bed again, I bet," Nate said.

"I miss my dolls."

"And not your brother?" Winona teased.

Evelyn grew thoughtful. "Funny thing, Ma. When Zach was living at home, the two of us spatted like cats and dogs. But now that he's gone, I sort of miss him."

Winona grinned. "It's normal to miss someone you love. When your father and I are apart, there is a great emptiness in my heart." She squeezed Nate's hand and had hers squeezed in return.

"Maybe we can pay Zach and Louisa a visit when we get back, Ma."

"I would like that very much, little one."

Nate was thinking of the council, of how much rested on their decision. The future of his family, the future of the Sa-gah-lee. He didn't realize Evelyn had said something until she yanked on his arm.

"Pa? Aren't you listening? I want you to take ma and me with you when you go off to fight the cannibals."

"Out of the question, princess."

"But what if something happens to you? Ma and I will be stuck here. The Sa-gah-lee will never let us go."

"Your mother is a resourceful woman. She'll get you out of here." But the question had Nate wondering. What would the remaining Sa-gah-lee do if most of their warriors were slain? Would they take out their rage and thirst for revenge on his wife and daughter?

"I would rather you made it back alive," Winona said. The truth was, she couldn't conceive of life without him. Nate meant everything to her. He was her life, her happiness, her reason for living. If he were to die, part of her would die with him.

They were nearing the center of the city, where the destruction was most evident. For every building still intact, four were in ruin. Large blocks were strewn everywhere. To their left a gigantic splintered beam jutted from a shattered roof like an accusing finger. Lengthening shadows lent an ominous air, courtesy of the sinking sun.

"Can we head back?" Evelyn asked uneasily.

"Sure," Nate said, and started to turn.

To the east a tremendous babble of voices pealed, swelling to a crescendo of whoops and savage yells. Shrieks and screams echoed down the man-made canyons, as if the Sa-gah-lee were running amok.

Evelyn clutched Nate's shirt. "What in the world are they doing? What's it all about, Pa?"

Nate couldn't say. But if filled him with misgiving. Perhaps Broken Stick had prevailed. Perhaps the Sa-gah-lee were coming to make good on Broken Stick's threat to have him staked out for the cannibals.

The bedlam was growing louder by the second.

"It sounds as if they're headed this way," Evelyn declared.

That it did. Nate glanced at Winona. "Take Evelyn and hide."

"Why? What do you know that I do not?"

Around a corner a hundred yards away swept scores of Sa-gah-lee, primarily warriors. Their cries rose to the clouds, and they swooped down the street like barbarians on a rampage.

Nate automatically stepped in front of Winona and

Evelyn, prepared to sacrifice his life to defend their own.

Like surf crashing onto a rocky shore, the Great Ones swept to a stop only yards away, and from their ranks strode their leader. Ezriah Hampton was at his heels. Hawk marched up to Nate, clasped him by the shoulders, and uttered several words.

"Translate for me," Nate told the trapper.

"That's why he dragged me along," Ezriah groused, then grinned. "You should be right pleased, hoss. The council is over. They've made their decision." His grin expanded. "The Sa-gah-lee are going to war."

Chapter Eleven

Ezriah Hampton wasn't grinning the next morning. He was scowling and swearing and waving his spindly arms as he railed at Nate King. "How dare you! When I said you were sneaky, I had no idea! Damn you all to hell! What you did isn't right! It isn't fair! Going to Hawk behind my back! If I told you once, I told you ten times! I don't want to go! Do you hear me? Fight your war without me!"

Nate had been waiting for the old trapper to pause to catch his breath, and now he answered in a reasonable tone. "I'm sorry, Ezriah. Sincerely. But I need you. Winona doesn't speak their tongue as well as you do, and with so many lives at risk I can't afford mistakes. It has to be you."

Ezriah's eye jerked and twitched as if fit to explode. "Like hell it does! I don't want to die helping these people! They've held me prisoner for twenty years! *Twenty years!* I'd as soon see the stinking cannibals wipe them out as the other way around! Tell Hawk you've changed your mind."

"I can't."

"You're a bastard, Nate King. A deceitful, no-account bastard. I hope the Dabi-muzza eat you clear down to the bone."

Nate forgave the insults. Under the circumstances, he couldn't blame the man. "I'll do my best to ensure no harm comes to you."

Ezriah was beet red with fury. "Don't try to butter me up with promises you can't keep! There's nothing you can do that will guarantee my safety."

"I can have Hawk pick five warriors to stay at your side at all times."

"Five or fifty, it won't make a difference. The cannibals will get me. I just know it!" Ezriah gave a little shudder. "Call it a premonition. Call it whatever you want. But I've had a feeling for years now that one day the Dabi-muzza would get their hands on me, and that will be that."

"Our futures are never set in stone. A lot of times we fret over things that never come to pass. To borrow some of your own words, worry is as useless as teats on a boar."

"I wish to hell I was a boar. I'd gore you to death for what you've done."

Winona witnessed the exchange but held her tongue. She felt sorry for Hampton, but her husband had only done what had to be done. "Nate has our best interest at heart, Ezriah. With your help, the Sa-gah-lee will succeed. Then they will set us free."

"Oh, sure, lady. All I have to do is live through a damn *war!* Easy as can be." The trapper snorted in disgust and stomped over to his corner. "I hate all of you! I hope your man dies!" Turning his back to them, he sank down, a study in despair.

147

"Maybe I should talk to him, Ma," Evelyn whispered. "I can cheer him up."

"Mr. Hampton needs some time to himself," Winona said, and glanced out the window. The sun was an hour high in a cloudless sky. "It will not be long now, husband."

Nate nodded. The war party was due to leave at midmorning. A precaution in case any cannibals had lingered near the mesa after sunrise, as they occasionally did to waylay unsuspecting Sa-gah-lee. Taking Winona in his arms, he kissed her forehead. "Try not to worry too much. I can handle myself pretty well, remember?"

"Do not get cocky. Even the best of warriors can be brought low by chance or the mistakes of others."

Smiling, Nate kissed her again. "Careful, or you'll become a worrywart like Ezriah." He embraced her tightly, praying he lived to do it a thousand more times before he met his Maker.

"Pa, we have company," Evelyn announced.

Hawk stood in the doorway. Behind him were Stone and Antelope. The leader addressed Hampton, and Ezriah gestured as if telling Hawk to leave him be. But Hawk took a step into the room, sternly repeating what he had said.

Sighing, the trapper stiffly rose. "The chief says he wants to show you something, King. Says it's important. Says it might help you. I have to go to translate." He swore luridly. "Makes me sorry I ever learned the stupid language."

Time was short and they had to hurry. Hawk guided them into the heart of the lost city, to a building that had been devastated by the cataclysm.

"Beats me what he's up to," Ezriah remarked. "The tribe never uses this area, that I know of."

Nate followed Hawk through a jagged opening in a wall, past piles of debris, to a bare spot on the floor about four feet square. A metal ring was encased in the wood. Seizing it, Hawk pulled, raising a trapdoor that creaked on hinges long neglected.

"I'll be jiggered!" Ezriah exclaimed. "I never knew this was here."

Stone produced a torch from a niche in an adjoining wall and lit it using quartz from his pouch. Holding the torch aloft, he descended a short flight of steps.

Hawk motioned for Nate to go next.

Ducking his head and swiping at a spiderweb, Nate went down. To one side were dusty shelves lined with clay containers, the majority of which were cracked and broken. On the other side was an incredible sight.

Ezriah was just as stunned. "Tell me I'm dreaming! All these years and I never guessed! God, I could have fought my way out long ago!"

It was a chest-high mound of personal effects and sundry articles. There were rifles, pistols, knives, swords, daggers, ammunition pouches, powder horns, and possibles bags. There were shirts, pants, hats, boots, shoes, blankets, coffeepots, and tin plates. As well as parfleches, leggings, buckskin dresses, moccasins, strings of beads, tomahawks, lances, bows, and hide shields.

Hawk seemed pleased by Nate's reaction. "We have collected these from many captives over many winters," Hampton translated. "Since you are white men, I thought you would be happier with white weapons. You may help yourselves. Take whatever you want."

Nate saw the stock of a Hawken sticking from the pile and tugged. Other than a layer of dust, the rifle was in perfect condition. "There's enough here to outfit an army. Why haven't the Sa-gah-lee used these to fight the Dabi-muzza?"

"We do not know how to make thundersticks work," Hawk said. "Even if we did, it is bad medicine to use anything belonging to anyone the cannibals eat. That is why we do not always bring weapons or other items

David Thompson

back with us, why we threw your woman's thunder-sticks and the one belonging to your daughter into the spring."

"Do you still have our horses?"

"Two are still alive."

"The others died?"

"They were cut up and used in the soup you have been eating."

"Oh."

"It is rare for us to acquire horses. Usually they are hard to control and run off. We had hoped the Dabi-muzza would show an interest in them and eat their flesh instead of ours, but they did not."

Ezriah had helped himself to a fine flintlock pistol and was caressing the smooth barrel as if it were a lover's limb. "This is nicer than the ones I had when they jumped me." Suddenly bending, he grabbed a pair of buckskin pants and held them against his legs. "Look! They'll fit! I don't have to traipse around half naked anymore!"

Hawk started up the steps. "I must attend to other preparations. Stone will stay with you."

Nate had a request to make. "With your permission, I'd like to give my wife and daughter weapons." So they could defend themselves if worse came to worst.

"I would gladly let you. But Broken Stick and some others will cause trouble if they find out. It is best for now if you do not. After we have defeated the Dabi-muzza, it will be different."

"Can I give them other things? Blankets, for instance?"

"As you wish." Smiling, Hawk climbed on out.

Ezriah was yanking items from the pile as fast as he could, examining those that caught his fancy and discarding others, cackling the whole while. "Look at this dagger! It's Spanish, or I'm the Queen of England! The hilt is inlaid with gems! I bet it's worth a fortune." He

150

snatched up another object. "And this leather pouch! It's got an emblem of some kind." Flipping the pouch open, he shoved his hand inside. When he pulled it out, gold coins filled his palm. "Lordy! Will you look at this!"

"Gold won't help us against the cannibals," Nate noted. "You can come back for it later."

"Like hell," Ezriah said, and tittered inanely. "From now on, where I go, this goes!"

Nate leaned the Hawken against a wall and sorted through the mound. Of the dozens of pistols he selected four of the newest. It was too much to expect to find a Bowie, but he did come across a double-edged knife with an eighteen-inch steel blade and an ivory hilt. Testing the heft, he swung it a few times.

A pair of smaller knives caught Nate's eye, so slender they could easily be concealed up a woman's sleeve. He also chose a couple of derringers and a short-barreled flintlock.

Two ammo pouches and two powder horns were added to Nate's growing pile. So were four Hudson's Bay blankets and two parfleches.

A glint of metal buried amid the booty drew Nate's hand to a peculiar cylinder. Peculiar, that was, until Nate pulled it out and realized what it was. "A spyglass!" he declared. The lenses were intact. Extending the sections, he raised it to his eye and trained it up through the trapdoor. It worked perfectly.

Among Nate's other discoveries was another parfleche, crammed with pemmican that was still edible, and a possibles bag in a lot better shape than his own. He transferred his fire steel and flint and other effects into it and slung it across his chest.

Careful to keep his back to Stone, Nate placed the small knives, the two derringers, and the short-barreled flintlock in the folds of one of the blankets. He wrapped an ammo pouch and powder horn in another, then stacked the four blankets and set the telescope and the other ammo pouch and powder horn on top. The four pistols went under his belt. That left the Hawken, which he cradled in the crook of his right arm.

"What do you think, hoss? How do I look?"

Nate swiveled toward Hampton. He hadn't been paying particular attention to what the trapper was doing, and for several seconds he was struck speechless with astonishment.

"Well?" Ezriah goaded. He had stripped off his old shirt and the breechclout, replacing them with the buckskin pants he had found and a broad-sleeved purple shirt that had been in style decades ago. Over the shirt he wore a red velvet coat with a row of shiny brass buttons down the front. On his feet were high-heeled knee-high square-toed black boots more fitting for the French court than the frontier. A broad-brimmed Spanish-style hat crowned his white mane, and from his slim shoulders hung a blue cloak decorated with yellow trim along the lower hem and white lace at the throat. Buckled to his skinny waist was an ornate curved sword as long as he was tall. Over his arm was slung the pouch containing the gold. And in his left hand was a Kentucky rifle. "Do you think I cut a dashing figure?"

"People would notice you anywhere," Nate said.

Ezriah construed it as a compliment. "Wish I had a mirror. These are the grandest clothes I've ever had on. I'd like to see how I look." He swirled the cloak with a flourish. "Can you imagine me strolling through St. Louis in this getup? I'd have women falling all over me."

"You're going to war dressed like that?"

"Sure. Why not?" Ezriah looked down at himself. "Oh. I'll stick out like a sore thumb in the woods, won't I? Well, I don't care. If I've got to die, this is the kind of outfit I want to be buried in."

Nate saw there was no talking him out of it. "Suit yourself. But shouldn't you take a pistol or two? That sword won't help much if the cannibals get in close."

"How stupid do you think I am?" Ezriah retorted, and swept his cloak back to reveal a flintlock on either hip, tucked under his wide brown leather belt. "And I'm taking an ammo pouch and powder horn, too."

Stone moved to the steps and made a comment.

"He says we can't stay much longer. It'll be time for the war party to head out soon."

Nate gave the mound a last scrutiny and spotted a strip of fabric bearing white and blue flowers. Curious, he slipped it loose and discovered it was a small bonnet.

"That'll look fetching on you," Ezriah said, and roared with mirth.

Stone insisted they leave, and lowered the trapdoor behind them.

They hastened off, Nate thankful the warrior hadn't inspected the blankets. He was betraying Hawk's trust, but it couldn't be helped. Winona's and Evelyn's safety came before all else.

Both were waiting in the doorway of their dwelling. Nate wanted to slip by them, but they were riveted in amazement by the one-eyed peacock.

Ezriah assumed a flamboyant pose, his hat at a rakish slant, his cloak bunched over one shoulder, a hand on the hilt of his sword. Displaying his yellow teeth, he said, "What do you think, ladies?"

Evelyn put a hand to her throat. "Why, Mr. Hampton, you're downright beautiful!"

"Thank you, little maiden. And you, Mrs. King?"

The only thing that kept Winona from laughing was the knowledge that his feelings would be hurt. "You are walking rainbow," she said diplomatically.

"I knew it!" Ezriah crowed.

The Flathead women appeared at the window and had the decency not to say what their twinkling eyes betrayed they were thinking.

Nate pushed past his wife and daughter and over

against the far wall, catching Winona's attention as he passed her. She brought Evelyn over, and the three of them hunkered.

"Where did you find all this?"

"The Sa-gah-lee have a secret cache," Nate said, and gave explicit directions on how to find it. "I brought a blanket for all four of you. Don't unfold them until we leave. Hidden in the bottom two are some weapons. If I don't make it back, go to the cache. Arm yourselves with rifles and whatever else you'll need and make your escape."

"Don't talk like that, Pa," Evelyn said. "You'll make it back. I know you will."

"Almost forgot," Nate said, handing her the bonnet. "This is for you."

"How pretty!" Evelyn squealed, and tried it on.

From outside Ezriah hollered, "Don't dawdle, big man! Stone says we have to get cracking."

For what might be the final time, Nate hugged his daughter, then his wife. Gazing tenderly into her eyes, he said softly, "Whatever happens, know that I love you with all my heart and soul, and always will. You are the best wife any man could ever have."

"And you, husband," Winona said, choked with emotion, "are the kind of man a woman is proud to call her own."

Nate's eyes were threatening to mist over. Wheeling, he stalked out and fell into step beside Stone, who was eager to reach the public square.

Ezriah swaggered along as if he were a prince. He kept squinting up at the sun and finally observed, "I forgot how blamed hot it's been. I'm roasting like a pig on a spit."

"Maybe you should shed the cloak and the coat," Nate recommended.

"Not on your life. I'd rather sweat to death."

The war party had gathered near the platform. Hawk

was going from warrior to warrior, verifying that they were ready, his face and arms painted with bold red stripes.

Fully the entire tribe was on hand to see the warriors off. All one hundred and fourteen Sa-gah-lee. Of that number, forty-seven were women and twenty-nine were children. That left thirty-eight men. And since ten were staying behind under Stone, the war party was composed of twenty-seven warriors, including Hawk.

Counting Nate and Ezriah, the total was twenty-nine.

"Not much of an army, is it?" the old trapper remarked.

"It will have to do," Nate said. He had advised Hawk to have every warrior bring a bow *and* a lance, and he was pleased to see they had obeyed.

"What if you're wrong, big man?"

"About what?"

"About how many Dabi-muzza there are. About how close their lair is. About everything. Do you realize what you've done?" Ezriah waved a hand toward the Sa-gah-lee. "You've doomed them. If most of their menfolk are killed, it's only a matter of time before the cannibals overrun the rest."

"What do you care? I thought you hated them."

"Yeah, well—" Ezriah said, and fell silent.

"You faker," Nate said, chuckling. "You do have feelings for them. You're just too proud to admit it."

Hawk came over. A quiver and bow were across his back, a lance in his left hand. "We are ready," he said through Hampton, and nodded at four men who had large pouches slung over a shoulder. "As you wanted, we have brought all the dried meat and extra food my people have. Enough to last all of us several sleeps."

"Good," Nate said. Several sleeps was more than enough time to find where the cannibals lived. Especially since they could move faster now that they need not waste valuable time hunting game as they went. "What about the two horses?"

"They are being brought even as we speak."

Nate hoped to use the horses to rove ahead of the war party and scout around. But when the horses were led up, he was horrified to find they were literal skin and bones. "Haven't you been feeding them?"

"Some of the women go down each day and gather grass," Hawk said.

"They're not getting anywhere near enough. You should picket them in the high grass each morning and leave them there all day. Otherwise they'll die on you before too long."

"So?"

"So they won't—" Nate said, and stopped when it hit him that the Great Ones *wanted* the animals to keel over so they could eat them. "They are of no use to me in their condition. I will go on foot like the rest of you."

A tragic mood gripped the crowd as the war party headed across the square. Women wailed and gnashed their teeth for husbands they were certain were going to their doom. Children bawled for fathers they were certain they would never see again. The whole tribe dogged them as far as the east gate, and waved and wept as the war party disappeared down the mouth of the tunnel.

Nate, Ezriah, and Hawk were the final three. Nate glanced back and was deeply touched to see Winona and Evelyn among the Sa-gah-lee, both bravely smiling and waving. He responded in kind to reassure them. Then he pivoted on his heel and descended into the tunnel's shadowed confines.

"I still can't believe you're dragging me along," Ezriah complained. "If anything happens to me, I swear I'll rise up from the dead and haunt you."

They didn't bother with torches. When they reached the bottom, Nate had Hawk line the warriors up in pairs while he searched for sign. He found cannibal tracks leading away from the mesa, but not toward the east end of the valley as he expected. The tracks bore to the north, toward the mountains.

Hawk was also puzzled. "What are the Dabi-muzza up to? There is only one way in and out of the valley."

"That you know of," Nate said.

Another perplexing discovery awaited them where the high grass ended. A well-worn trail led up a steep slope into dense forest.

"Ezriah and I will go on ahead by ourselves," Nate proposed. "Give us a little head start, then follow. Keep the men as quiet as you can."

Broken Stick immediately objected. "What is to stop the white-eye from circling around and going back for his wife and child?" he snapped at Hawk. "Two or three of us must be with him at all times."

"He has given his word, and that is enough for me," Hawk said. "But to make you happy I will send Antelope and Growing Grass along."

The two warriors were not particularly enthusiastic about the notion, but they glued themselves to Nate as he climbed steadily higher and deeper into the foreboding range. The woods were ominously dark, wildlife disturbingly absent. They had gone perhaps a mile when a pale object to the left of the trail caught Nate's eye. It was partially buried, and he had to tug hard to extract a human arm bone showing abundant gnaw marks.

Antelope and Growing Grass hefted their lances and nervously scoured the adjacent slopes.

Nate pushed on, the trail winding along a sheer bluff and over a succession of ridges. Halting in aspens midway down a slope, he saw that the trail vanished in a narrow ravine mired in shadow. Outside the ravine, strewn at random, were human skulls and more bones— scores and scores of complete skeletons, the telescope

David Thompson

revealed—maybe hundreds, all told. And all the skulls had been bashed in, presumably so the cannibals could eat the brains.

"It is their lair!" Growing Grass whispered.

"Do not be so sure," Nate had the old trapper convey. "I have not seen any tracks of women or children. We will go down and investigate."

"Shouldn't we wait for Hawk and the others?" Antelope was quick to say.

Nate could tell that the pair were so scared they might run off if he left them alone with Ezriah. So he reluctantly agreed, and within half an hour the rest of the war party arrived. Nate consulted with Hawk, who had the warriors spread out, every man nocking an arrow to his bowstring.

At a wave of Nate's arm, they advanced in a skirmish line.

Nate had the Hawken's stock wedged to his shoulder. When they reached the bones, he motioned for the Great Ones to wait and went on alone. The ravine's high walls reared above him like the maw of a gargantuan beast. They were so high, sunlight rarely penetrated. Sidling to the left, he crouched to let his eyes adjust and presently beheld a recessed niche thirty feet away—and three bulky forms sprawled in sleep.

Retreating, Nate hurried to Hawk. "Have a few of your men throw stones into the ravine. Tell the rest to be ready. When I raise my arm overhead, they are to let their arrows fly. Instruct them to go for the head, not the body."

Tension crackled like lightning in a thunderstorm. Most of the Great Ones were scared and made no attempt to hide it. Some were poised to bolt as rocks were chucked into the defile. Not ten seconds after the first one was hurled, out into the sunlight shuffled a red-haired cannibal, befuddled by sleep and squinting against the glare.

Nate elevated his arm. Arrows buzzed like a swarm of angry bees, twenty-seven of them; a few sliced into the beast-man's shoulders and chest, but most were more accurate. The creature toppled without a sound, its head resembling a bloodstained pincushion.

Seconds later the other two Dabi-muzza burst into the open, shielding their eyes as they snarled and pumped their heavy spears. More arrows whizzed, warriors unleashing two or three shafts in swift succession. Riddled, the cannibals stumbled and fell and clawed at the dirt in their death throes.

One of them was missing a thumb and two fingers on his left hand.

Nate hadn't fired a shot. There had been no need. He smiled as the stunned warriors yipped and whooped and clapped one another on the back, elated at their victory.

Hawk was no exception. "Did you see how easy it was!" he cried, gripping Nate's arm. "You were right! In the daylight we have the advantage!" He howled in an excess of enthusiasm. "Lead us to the rest! We will slay them all!"

Ezriah Hampton, leaning on his rifle, snorted in ridicule and said in English, "Listen to the fool! Why don't you tell them the truth, King? Before this is over, a hell of a lot of us are going to die."

Chapter Twelve

Five hours later the mountains were at their backs and a broad plain had unfolded before the war party. On the far side—ten miles, by Nate King's reckoning—towered another range. The trail pointed straight toward it.

"That's where the beasties will be," Ezriah said.

Nate tended to agree. The ravine was a convenient spot for the Dabi-muzza to lie low during the day, near enough to the lost city so they could reach it shortly after sundown and waylay Sa-gah-lee tardy in returning home. Evidently, some of the captives were consumed at the ravine and others were borne northward. Food for the whole clan, Nate figured.

Hampton gazed at the sinking sun. "In case you ain't noticed, friend, we won't get there before nightfall. And I don't much like the thought of being caught in the open. The Death Devils will make mincemeat out of us."

Hawk stepped forward. "Why do we delay?"

"I can tell you," Broken Stick said. "For all his bluster,

the white-eye knows he has made a mistake. He knows that once the sun goes down, we will be at the mercy of the Dabi-muzza. We must hurry to the mesa before it is too late."

"It's already too late," Nate heard the trapper reply. "We'd never reach the city before dark. So we'll camp right here."

"Up in the trees would be better," Broken Stick said. "There is more cover."

"For the cannibals, too," Nate responded, and gave Hawk several suggestions the leader promptly carried out.

Half the men were sent up the slope with instructions to gather as much firewood as they could before night fell. The other half were set to digging a circle of pits. Each was roughly four feet in diameter and two feet deep, the circle itself approximately fifty feet in circumference. The diggers worked at a furious pace, spurred by the possible consequences if they were not done in time. Meanwhile, an enormous pile of firewood took shape in the center.

All that was left of the sun was a golden sliver when Hawk assembled the warriors and Nate had some fill the pits with wood while others made torches by wrapping layers of grass around suitable broken branches.

As twilight shrouded the wilderness a keening cry to the north forewarned the war party that the cannibals were abroad. Nate ordered six torches lit, and the warriors to stand ready with their lances.

Out of the gathering dark rose grunts and low growls.

"A band of Dabi-muzza on their way to the mesa," Nate said to Ezriah.

"Sounds like five or six of the demons," Hampton said. "And those torches aren't enough to keep them from attacking."

"I know. I want them to come in close."

"You do? Then you're crazier than I imagined. The

161

Sa-gah-lee will break and run, leaving you and me to be the main course at the next Death Devil get-together."

"Have a little faith, Ezriah."

"In who? You? Mister, I learned a long time ago that anyone who has faith in anything other than his own self is a natural-born jackass who doesn't have the brains God gave a turnip."

Movement beyond the pits materialized into a hulking brute who advanced from the north with a spear leveled in both knobby hands.

Hawk and some of the nearest warriors glanced at Nate, anxious to put the next stage in his plan into effect. But Nate was in no rush. "Hold your ground! Let the cannibals think you're afraid of them!"

"If they were any more afraid, they'd faint," Ezriah muttered.

Another squat shape hove out of the gloom, this time to the west. Then a third to the east. Growling ferociously, their thick lips pulled back from their fangs, they warily closed in.

"Now?" Hawk asked.

"Not yet," Nate answered.

The creatures were almost to the pits. If they noticed the firewood, they didn't seem to care it was there. Another few yards and they started to enter the circle to get at the Sa-gah-lee.

"Now?" Hawk said again.

"No."

The warriors holding the torches, anxiously waiting for their signal, had eyes only for Nate. The rest had their lances cocked to throw.

Ezriah thumbed back the hammer on his rifle. "What are you waiting for? Another couple of seconds and those critters will be close enough to pee on us."

The creature to the north had just passed a pit. It beady eyes were agleam with a craving for flesh, its grotesque visage twisted in malevolent intent.

"Torches!" Nate bawled, and the instant Hampton re-layed his command, three warriors hurled torches at fire pits nearest the three creatures. The dry wood instantly ignited and flames flared high.

The cannibals recoiled, shielding their eyes from the glare.

"Lances, now!" Nate thundered, and four warriors rushed each of the Dabi-muzza. Sixteen lances cleaved the night. At that distance only one missed, and the creatures fell with their craniums cored, dead before they realized what had occurred.

Again Sa-gah-lee victory cries pealed long and loud. Protected by friends, those who had thrown their lances retrieved them.

At Nate's urging, the bodies were dragged beyond the fire pits to make it easier for other Dabi-muzza to claim them. He had learned his lesson well the other night. The cannibals had no compunctions about de-vouring their own kind. Where horses hadn't worked as bait, dead Dabi-muzza just might. And soon his idea was put to the test.

Piercing shrieks announced the arrival of additional creatures, who shunned the glow of the fire pits as they roved back and forth.

Nate directed Hawk to have a fourth pit set ablaze on the south side as an extra precaution.

"Even if your harebrained plan works," Ezriah said, "how much time will it buy us? An hour? Two at the most?"

"There's no predicting," Nate said. But any attempt to stave off a concerted attack was worth it, in his es-timation.

The next half an hour frayed everyone's nerves. Fully a dozen spectral figures surrounded them, constantly snarling and grunting and thumping their chests. Sev-

eral ventured into the light but always immediately re-
treated again.

Then, in a rush, a pair of Dabi-muzza bounded out
of the night, seized the ankles of the dead creature to
the north, and dragged it off. Since the Sa-gah-lee made
no attempt to interfere, the rest of the cannibals lost no
time hauling off the other dead ones. Their grunts re-
ceded into the distance, and soon all that could be heard
was the sighing of the wind.

"I'll be damned," Ezriah said. "It worked."

Nate wasn't satisfied until an hour had gone by and
the creatures had failed to reappear. Sentries were
posted near each fire pit with orders to keep the flames
burning bright. Everyone else was treated to jerked deer
meat and roots. Everyone except Nate, who ate some of
the pemmican he had found in the underground cache.

"I've got to hand it to you, friend," Ezriah said,
munching noisily. "You're as clever as a fox. But the
real test will be tomorrow."

That it would, Nate agreed. Daylight or not, the Dabi-
muzza were not about to let themselves be extermi-
nated. They would resist tooth and claw, and fight all
the fiercer with their women and offspring menaced.

"Tell Hawk the men should take turns sleeping,"
Nate said. "Half at a time."

Hawk's reply caused Hampton to chuckle. "He says
you must be suffering from sunstroke. No one will be
able to sleep knowing the cannibals are out there."

"They have to try," Nate insisted. They couldn't wage
war effectively if they were bone-tired. To set an example, he lay on his back with an arm across his eyes,
emptied his mind of worries, and tried to doze off.
Truly tried. But an hour or so later he was still wide
awake, and almost glad when a bestial shriek gave him
an excuse to sit up.

"They're back," Ezriah mentioned the obvious. "Or
else it's a new bunch of ghouls."

No one else had even tried to get any sleep, Nate realized as he rose. He stepped to where Hawk and Broken Stick were peering into the darkness in the direction of the latest cry. "See anything?"

"Not yet," Hawk said.

Guttural grunts confirmed there was more than one. The creatures started circling the camp and occasionally let out with nerve-jangling screeches.

"This is going to be a long night, young coon," Ezriah said.

That it was. For hours the cannibals lurked in the darkness, never coming near enough to be seen, never venturing within range of the war party's arrows or lances. The warriors were in a constant state of intense dread; not a man among them enjoyed a single moment's rest.

"What are they waiting for?" Hawk wondered, along about four in the morning. "Why don't they attack?"

Nate couldn't say, but he'd wager it was a combination of factors. The fire pits, which the Sa-gah-lee kept aflame at all times, and the deaths of the other three earlier, which had shown the Dabi-muzza what would happen if they ventured in too close. At any rate, he was supremely glad when the faint glow of impending sunrise silenced the inhuman cries and bearish grunts.

"They've lit a shuck for home!" Ezriah happily declared. He had pulled his cloak around him to ward off the predawn chill.

As word spread, joy etched every countenance. So did fatigue. Nate had a decision to make—namely, should they push on at daybreak or try to sleep for several hours? He posed the question to Hawk.

"We push on," the leader said without hesitation. "My warriors are eager to end it. Eager to live as other tribes do. Without fear, without shame."

As soon as the sun crested the horizon the Sa-gah-lee were on the move. The trail took them across the plain to the next mountain range, to stark, foreboding peaks, their lower slopes sparsely covered with vegetation. Jumbled boulders and talus fields littered the upper reaches. Remote and desolate, the range had little to offer man or beast.

Nate was no geologist, but the impression he had was of great age. The mountains were ancient, perhaps the oldest on the continent, all the more fitting as a haven for creatures from the dawn of time.

The trail seared the slope above like a diagonal scar, worn inches into the earth by the tread of innumerable feet over the vastness of centuries.

"What's that smell?" Ezriah asked.

Nate sniffed. The putrid odor characteristic of the cannibals clung to the trail like the reek of manure to a farmer's boots. Additional proof, as if any were needed, that here, indeed, was the lair of the Dabi-muzza. He began to climb.

"You'd best pray there's not two hundred of them up there," Ezriah said. "Or this will be our last day on earth."

The trail wound around the slope and along a shelf to a wide cleft in a low cliff. The stench was particularly strong, and Nate breathed shallow as he entered. He had gone a couple of feet when the old trapper whispered his name.

The warriors had halted. Except for Hawk and a few of the bravest, they were pale and slick with sweat.

"We should turn back before it is too late," Broken Stick whispered.

By their expressions a lot of others were inclined to agree. To forestall a mass desertion, Nate said in contempt, "If you care so little for your people, go ahead."

Predictably, Broken Stick bristled. "No one cares for the Sa-gah-lee more than I do!"

"Then prove it," Nate challenged, and gazed along the line of pasty faces. "Stand up to the Dabi-muzza.

Stop them from ever eating another human being. If you don't, you must live with the decision for the rest of your lives. Every time you hear the screams of a loved one being devoured, you will think back to this day and regret your cowardice." So saying, he rotated and stalked into the cleft, the Hawken cocked, his senses primed. He didn't look to see if they followed. If they didn't, so be it.

The high walls blocked out the sun, but enough light filtered down to reveal a few bones that might crack like dry twigs and give Nate away if he stepped on them. He advanced cautiously, the cleft narrowing with every stride. At the other end it was barely wider than his shoulders. Stopping, he poked his head out.

A wide earthen ramp led down into a hollow or basin carved by erosion out of solid rock. Hundreds of yards from end to end, it was hemmed by towering heights that perpetually shrouded it in twilight shadow. At the near end were piles and piles of bones, some added so recently they gleamed white, others yellowed with age.

Beyond were the cannibals, three dozen or better, mostly adult males and females. The women had the same stocky builds and bestial features as the men. There were also eight or nine little ones ranging in age from only a few years to fourteen or fifteen. All were dressed in crude hides. Some were resting. Some were conversing in their guttural dialect. One male was sharpening a heavy spear using a jagged rock.

The three dead cannibals lay near the far wall. Next to them, bound hand and foot, were two Indians, a young man and a woman. Both had been stripped naked.

As Nate looked on, a pair of female cannibals squatted in front of the woman and poked at her legs with their thick, blunt fingers. She tried to pull away but had nowhere to go. Suddenly a female cannibal bent down and bit into her thigh. The woman screamed in mortal terror, her cry echoing and reechoing off the rock ramparts. On hearing it, other cannibals moved toward her.

Breakfast was being served.

"What the hell is going on?" Ezriah whispered.

Nate turned. The entire war party lined the cleft. "A woman is being eaten," he revealed, courtesy of the trapper. "I do not know what tribe she is from, but she could be from yours. Do we stand here and do nothing? Or do we show the Dabi-muzza that we are men?"

Angry murmurs demonstrated their intent.

"I'll go first," Nate said. "Spread out with your bows ready, and watch for my signal. Go for the head, not the body."

Another scream pealed as Nate dashed down the dirt ramp. Almost all the cannibals had turned toward the captives, and none saw him.

Out of the cleft streamed the warriors, each as grim as death. They fanned to either side, arrows notched, their lances wedged under the straps that held their quivers in place. Hawk and Broken Stick were on Nate's right, Antelope, Growing Grass, and Stars at Night to his immediate left. With a start, he realized Ezriah wasn't there, and glanced over his shoulder.

The trapper was framed in the cleft, smirking slyly. "I told you, hoss! I'm not taking part in your damned fool war. I'll wait back yonder."

"Ezriah, no—!" Nate said, but the cantankerous coot was gone.

A howl of outrage arose at the far end of the basin. A female cannibal had spotted the war party.

The captives were forgotten as the Dabi-muzza snatched up spears and rocks and surged across the basin in a body, the males moving to the front, the women next, the young ones bringing up the rear. Halting about a hundred yards out, they vented a feral chorus of roars and shrieks, the males stomping their feet and thumping their broad chests, the women screeching like hags, the youngsters imitating them.

The display of pure and total savagery was enough to intimidate anyone, and Nate wasn't surprised when several of the warriors started to back toward the ramp. Without Hampton, he couldn't ask them to stand firm. Fortunately, Hawk did it for him. But whether they would hold their ground when the creatures charged was another question.

A large cannibal had moved out in front and was pounding and stomping in a frenzy. It occurred to Nate that the Dabi-muzza were working themselves up to a fever pitch of raw bloodlust and would soon hurtle forward in an unstoppable tidal wave of brawn and fangs.

Some of the warriors were quaking in fright. One man bolted and didn't stop even when Hawk yelled at him.

Something had to be done to bolster their resolve or they would all break and flee.

Nate sighted down the Hawken, fixing a bead on the large brute's forehead. He held his breath to steady his aim and smoothly stroked the trigger. At the retort, the muzzle belched lead and smoke. The large male staggered, raised a brawny hand to the cavity in its brow, and oozed to earth like so much melted wax.

It had the desired effect. The Sa-gah-lee whooped and hollered out of all proportion to the deed, which was fine by Nate so long as it bolstered their courage.

Across the basin the cannibals had fallen silent. Several males approached the fallen figure and nudged it with their spears. When one uttered a rasping yowl, a collective roar reverberated and the Dabi-muzza charged, loping like wolves in long bounds that covered the distance astoundingly swiftly.

Nate was hastily reloading. He yanked the ramrod from its housing under the barrel, then paused. Hawk and the others were waiting for him to give the signal.

Thrusting his arm overhead, he marked the range. Ninety yards. Eighty yards. Seventy. Screeching hideously, the creatures frothed at the lips as if they were rabid.

Another second, and Nate's arm flashed down. Twenty-seven shafts whizzed in flight, arcing into the foremost ranks. Half a dozen fell, transfixed through the skull. Three times as many were wounded. But all it did was slow the cannibals slightly, not stop them. And it incensed them even further.

Nate whipped his arm once more and resumed reloading. Again a volley of arrows tore into the Dabimuzza. More fell, but not enough, nowhere near enough, and now they were only forty yards away, roiling in seething fury.

A last volley was unleashed and more cannibals—primarily males—dropped right and left. But plenty of creatures were left, and in a fierce torrent they flowed past the piles of bones and crashed into the wall of warriors.

Nate finished and swept up the Hawken. Simultaneously a cannibal filled the sights and he fired at point-blank range.

Men and man-eaters were grappling for their lives. Dropping the rifle, Nate jerked two of his pistols, his thumbs curling back the hammers as he drew. He shot a creature about to spear Hawk, pivoted, and cored the cranium of another.

Bedlam reigned. Sa-gah-lee and Dabi-muzza battled hand-to-hand, lances and knives against thick spears and sharp rocks, in a mad swirl of brutal combat. Screams, yells, curses, and roars eclipsed cries of the wounded and dying.

Nate had two loaded flintlocks left. Palming them, he sidestepped a streaking spear and downed the cannibal who had thrown it. He saw Growing Grass being throttled by a husky brute and spun to help him. Suddenly

170

his right arm was jarred by a blow to his wrist, and his pistol fell from fingers gone numb.

The female who had struck him was as massive as the males, and as hideous. Bulging muscles rippled as she slashed a rock at his throat.

In a glittering arc Nate flashed the double-edged knife from its scabbard. The razor edge bit into the she-brute's wrist, shearing sinew and bone, and her hand flopped at their feet. Instead of collapsing in shock and pain, she screeched and flung herself at him, her other hand balled into a fist, battering at his head and face.

Knocked backward, Nate saw her mouth yawn wide and her fangs swoop toward his throat. He drove the knife up and in and heard her strangled gurgle as the foot and a half of cold steel penetrated her vitals. Most foes would have crumbled, but such was the beast-woman's indomitable vitality that she clamped her remaining hand around his neck and sought to choke the life from him while her fangs gaped nearer.

Bent backward by her bulk and greater weight, Nate twisted the knife upward to try and pierce her heart. She hissed, her spittle flecking his face, his forearm growing slick with her blood and gore. Then, as she was about to sink her teeth into him, she stiffened and threw back her head. The next moment her legs buckled and she sank to her knees, scarlet ribbons seeping from her nose.

Wrenching the knife free, Nate shifted. Bodies were everywhere, the majority Dabi-muzza. Nearby lay Growing Grass, his throat a mangled ruin. Farther away was Runs Slow, a spear stuck in his ribs. Broken Stick was flopping like a fish out of water, his left arm ripped from its socket.

Other warriors and monstrosities were still locked in mortal struggle, and Nate moved to help the Sa-gah-lee. Hardly had he taken a step when a small bundle of ferocity tore into him, raining a rock at his legs and hips.

It was a child, a girl no older than Evelyn, her visage every bit as gruesome as her elders and lit by the same fanatical hatred. He countered the flurry, then sprang out of reach, his mind balking at the thought of slaying her. But she had no such reservations. Uttering a high-pitched wail, the girl pounced, swinging her rock at his knees.

Just then there was a blur of motion and a thud, and the girl was brought up short by an arrow jutting from her torso. Snarling, she took another step, her rock upraised. A second arrow transfixed her a finger's width from the first, punching her backward, and she sprawled across an older female. Perhaps her mother.

Nate glanced to his left. Antelope and several other warriors were on the ramp, picking off remaining cannibals with their bows. Antelope smiled, then trained his shafts on another target.

In less than a minute only a few severely wounded Dabi-muzza were left. Hawk and other Sa-gah-lee moved among them, dispatching them quickly with lances.

The slaughter was terrible to survey. Of the twenty-seven warriors who had entered the hollow only four-teen were still alive, and half were hurt. Of the cannibals, not one remained. The day of the Dabi-muzza was over.

Or was it? At he far end of the cleft a rifle boomed. "Ezriah!" Nate cried, and raced up the ramp. He envisioned the trapper being overwhelmed by cannibals who must have made it out alive, but when he shot into the sunlight Ezriah was twenty yards away, tendrils of smoke curling from the muzzle of his Kentucky rifle. Halfway between them lay a lone Dabi-muzza, a girl younger than the one Antelope had slain.

Ezriah looked up. "Damn you, Nate King. I said I wanted no part of your war."

Four days later, on a bright, crisp morning with sparrows chirping gaily in the pines, Nate stood beside Winona and Evelyn at the east end of the grassy valley. Great Ones filled the road behind them. Nearly every last man, woman, and child had come to see them off.

Hawk stepped forward and solemnly placed his palm on Nate's chest. "Friends forever. My people will never forget the service you have done them."

Done translating, Ezriah Hampton laughed. "Too bad we're leaving. Stick around long enough and I reckon they'd make you their god."

"We have a long way to go. Let's get started." Hand in hand with Winona and Evelyn, Nate started home.

Winona pressed against him, her joy boundless. "When we get back I plan to sleep for a week."

"Like hell you will, lady," Ezriah said. "First I've got a steak and pie coming, remember? After you've filled my belly you can snore away all you want."

Nate sighed. "Are you going to be like this the whole time?"

"Like what?" Ezriah innocently asked, and cackled like a madman.

AUTHOR'S NOTE

Of all the entries in the King Journal, those dealing with the red-haired cannibals in this volume and the Grandfather Of All Bears mentioned in the previous book are some of the more sensational. Certainly they are as hard to believe as the account of the NunumBi and the Lost Valley detailed earlier.

Initially, I decided not to transcribe them. I reasoned few would accept such incredible accounts.

Then I was reminded by a fellow historical buff and black powder enthusiast that the entries are a legitimate part of the journal, and as such, deserve to be related to contemporary readers to make of them what they will.

Perhaps he has a valid point. Stories of cannibals from the dawn of time and prehistoric bears as big as log cabins are no more far-fetched than the paranormal themes running rampant in the popular media.

Was Nate King sincere, or was he spinning a yarn? It is no secret Mountain Men delighted in telling tall tales. I leave it for you to decide.

WILDERNESS

Fang & Claw
David Thompson

To survive in the untamed wilderness a man needs all the friends he can get. No one can battle the continual dangers on his own. Even a fearless frontiersman like Nate King needs help now and then and he's always ready to give it when it's needed. So when an elderly Shoshone warrior comes to Nate asking for help, Nate agrees to lend a hand. The old warrior knows he doesn't have long to live and he wants to die in the remote canyon where his true love was killed many years before, slain by a giant bear straight out of Shoshone myth. No Shoshone will dare accompany the old warrior, so he and Nate will brave the dreaded canyon alone. And as Nate soon learns the hard way, some legends are far better left undisturbed.

___4862-0 $3.99 US/$4.99 CAN